Letters from a Wary Watcher
A Moira Edwards Walker Mystery

by

Rita Gard Seedorf and Margaret Albi Verhoef

Copyright 2016 by Rita Gard Seedorf and Margaret Albi Verhoef

For information, email Cozy Cat Press, cozycatpress@aol.com or visit our website at: www.cozycatpress.com

COZY CAT
PRESS

ISBN: 978-1-939816-85-6
Printed in the United States of America

Cover design by Paula Ellenberger
www.paulaellenberger.com

10 9 8 7 6 5 4 3 2 1

We dedicate this book to our children: Scott Michael Seedorf, Anna Seedorf Bollinger, Gretchen Verhoef Wanzenried and to our grandchildren: Roselyn Mae Wanzenried, Benjamin Henry Rose, and Alexander Thomas Rose.

Acknowledgments
For previewing the manuscript and generously giving their sage opinion: *Judy Crabb, Kerry Moxcey, Susan Whitman, and Gretchen Verhoef. For insights on growing up in Richland, Washington, near the Hanford Atomic Works: John and Jean Bruntlett and Richard Teals.* For their patience, love, and support, our husbands: *Martin Seedorf* and *Douglas Verhoef.* To *Martin Seedorf, retired EWU Professor of British History*, for hours of instruction on the early Cold War including the Cambridge Five Spy Ring and endless pots of strong coffee! And, of course, to *Patricia Rockwell* and the Cozy Cat Press.

Prologue

Does anyone really know his or her parents? If we feel safe as children, our parents are the gravity that holds our feet to the ground. We do not see them as separate from us. we relate to them only as they relate to us. We listen to the stories they tell and watch them interact with others. But do we really know them? We can neither go back in time and watch them play as children nor can we experience the world as it was when they were born. We can, however, read histories and works of fiction that allow us to gain some understanding of their lives.

I have spent much of my life trying to discover the truth about the secret work in which my mother, Moira Edwards Walker, was involved during World War II and in the immediate post war years, particularly her five-week disappearance during the holiday season of 1949-50. She never spoke a word about that time. The only clues to where she had been were the gifts she brought to my sister, my three cousins and me when she returned. Even though the five of us have moved many times during the more than 45 years that have passed since that day, we all still possess the special gift given to us by that diffident, polite and loving woman. She told us where she had been without saying a word when she presented each of us with an ancient scarab.

Scarabs are beetle-shaped amulets that were created in great numbers in Ancient Egypt. Like all amulets, they are believed to have the power to protect their owners from harm. Each of our sacred beetles is slightly different. She gave them to us in the order of our ages. The eldest, cousin William, received the largest, which is slightly more than one inch long. My sister Keiko, the youngest, was given the smallest scarab. Hers is slightly less than one half inch in length. Each of us has spent many hours of research in our desire to discover the special meaning of our particular stone. We have each created a story for our scarab and these stories have changed over the years as we learn more about Mother's activities.

Receiving our scarabs told us that Mother had been in Egypt but we were to learn nothing more about her clandestine activities until 1995 when the long held secret of the VENONA Intercepts was revealed to the public. The VENONA project was a successful attempt to decode and translate some of the highly encrypted cables sent from Soviet agents working in the United States to the KGB in Russia. The cables had been decoded between 1946 and 1980 but a cloak of secrecy was clapped around the project for 50 years.

In 1995, the first 49 of the thousands of intercepted, decrypted and translated cables from Soviet agents operating in the United States to Joseph Stalin's government in the 1940s were released. It was only with this knowledge that we were able to begin piecing together the story of deception, deceit, international espionage and betrayal in which my parents were involved. My sister, my cousins and I have long suspected that my parents had been involved in covert work. However, any time one of us questioned either of them, we were sternly told never to ask. Our curiosity grew with each refusal. Eventually we stopped asking and began researching the questions on our own.

Our move to Richland, Washington, in November of 1948 greatly concerned Aunt Margaret. As a physician, she and other health professionals were deeply concerned about the effects of emissions from nuclear production on those who worked at Hanford as well as those who live downwind of the plant. They had additional concerns about the effects on the Columbia River whose waters were used to cool the reactors.

We had learned a great deal about our mothers from two existing sets of letters that had been written between them. The first set covered the years 1937 to 1945 and the second set began in 1947 and ended in 1949.

Because the two women wrote of the past as well as the present, these letters offer a glimpse of the first six decades of the 20th century. Cousins Moira and Margaret Edwards were born in 1905, long before women were allowed to vote in either England or the United States. They were the only children of brothers who were both country doctors in the south of England. Margaret's parents immigrated to the United States before the beginning of World War I. Moira's parents had planned to join them but world events and a worldwide epidemic intervened, preventing them from reaching America. The history of both women was to be affected by World Wars I and II, the Cold War, and great strides in medicine, industry, nuclear warfare and technology.

I was nine-years-old and my sister, Keiko, was seven when we entered the life of Margaret Edwards Walker's family. The two of us remember happy childhoods even though the story of our first few years reads like a tragedy. I was born in Seattle, Washington, to hard working, consistent, and loving parents in the year 1934. Two years later, my sister joined our family. While she and I have different interests and ideas, I cannot imagine two more compatible sisters. We were inseparable, which proved to be of great benefit as we maneuvered through the many changes of our childhood years. We faced our challenges and opportunities together.

Keiko and I were five and seven years old respectively on Sunday, December 7, 1941, when the naval base at Pearl Harbor in the U.S. Territory of Hawaii was bombed by fighters, bombers, and torpedo planes launched from Japanese aircraft carriers. Four of the eight U.S. Navy battleships in the harbor were sunk and the others damaged. Cruisers, destroyers and training ships were also destroyed or disabled. Over 2,400 Americans were killed and nearly 1,200 others wounded.

The United States declared war on Imperial Japan the following day. Even though our Japanese-born parents had become American citizens, they were informed that they would be forced to abandon their Seattle home and business and move to an internment camp where our family would be housed in barracks apartments designed to allow each family 50 square feet of space per individual, one small window, one electrical socket and a wood stove. To save themselves and their daughters from such a fate, they sent Keiko and me away from them to live with a farm family in Sprague, Washington. They described it to us as a wonderful place with baby chicks and lambs and plenty of room to run and play. And that is how we saw it. We had each other, freedom to run, our own bedroom and plenty of food.

Two years later, we were once again relocated. We were invited to move to Spokane and become part of the Walker family where our cousin Yoshi was living and working at the time. Mr. Charles Walker was a journalist and his wife was a physician. It was very unusual at that time for a woman to have a professional career, particularly in the field of medicine. The Walkers and their three children, William, Bert, and

Catherine, welcomed us as family members and we instantly felt that we belonged there.

At the time we made this move from Sprague to Spokane, we had not seen our parents for some time and, sadly, we were never to see them again. Unable to bear the humiliation of being interned and, feeling secure that their daughters were in safe hands, they ended their lives. It must have been some time later that we were told. I remember feeling sad but not threatened. The Walker family had taken us in and wrapped themselves around us like a warm blanket.

The Walker house on West 14th Avenue was a wonderful place to grow up. It was like living in a fairy tale. Our room was on the top floor, which had been remodeled for Cousin Yoshi, who was the Walker children's nanny. Keiko and I shared a cozy bedroom just off the sitting room. We became a family of five children. William and Bert, who were the two oldest, did not ignore us as had the farm boys in our previous family.

Catherine was nearly a year older than I, and we three girls walked to school together and played all over the house and the neighborhood the rest of the time. At the end of the day we still wanted to giggle together. Either Yoshi or Dr. Walker, who we soon began to call Aunt Margaret, frequently were forced to send us to our respective bedrooms and command us to be silent.

We were eight around the dinner table when we were all home and nine when Uncle Charles' brother Thomas joined us, which he did at least once a week. None of us knew it at the time but a few years later he was to become Keiko's and my father. Another family member who we had not met but who was often discussed at the table was Aunt Margaret's cousin Moira, who lived in England.

The two corresponded regularly during the war and Moira's letters always caused much discussion. She first wrote from a war-torn village and later from London, sometimes while sitting or lying in a Morrison Shelter during a bombing raid. The Morrison was a table constructed of heavy steel with the sides closed in with wire mesh to protect her from falling debris. The shelter replaced the kitchen table in flats that had no garden. Those with enough land constructed Anderson shelters behind their homes.

Aunt Margaret and her cousin Moira had been close as children but had lost touch for twenty years. Their fathers, like Uncle Charles and my father Thomas, were brothers. However, unlike Uncle Charles and Thomas, who were journalists, they were both physicians. Expecting Moira's parents to follow them to Chicago, Margaret's mother and father bought a Chicago house large enough to house both families. However, world events prevented this plan from being fulfilled. The beginning of World War I in 1914 postponed their move. Moira and her parents survived the war but tragically, both parents passed away in the influenza epidemic, known as Swine Flu, that followed.

Moira was left on her own. She remained in school until she reached the school-leaving age of 14, after which she supported herself by becoming a 'maid-of-all-work' for several families. The two cousins completely lost contact until 1937 when Aunt Margaret received an unexpected letter. By that time she had become the mother of three children and was a practicing physician.

From that time on, Aunt Margaret supported and encouraged her cousin Moira in every way she could imagine. As Moira gained confidence and grew bolder and bolder, Aunt Margaret began to urge her to proceed with caution. From listening carefully to hushed conversations between our aunt and uncle we learned that Moira was in danger from much more than falling bombs. These conversations ended abruptly when they sensed that any of us were listening.

Shortly after Uncle Charles was called into active duty, his brother Thomas was sent to England. We three girls knew Thomas very well by then and decided that Moira and Thomas should meet in London and fall in love. One day William and Bert overheard us giggling about the two of them getting together and explained to us that millions and millions of people lived in England, moving around town was difficult and that we were being very silly.

However, the boys had underestimated their mother's powers. We soon got word that the two of them had met and were seeing each other from time to time. Here in America we called it dating. There in England they called it "walking out together." For some reason, we three girls broke out in fits of giggles whenever we heard that phrase. That "walking out together" led to Uncle Thomas surprising Moira with a proposal of marriage which she accepted. The two were married in February of 1943.

We girls laughed a lot but we worried too. We worried about our uncles Thomas and Charles, and we worried about the Moira we had never met. We occasionally heard that the father of one of our classmates had been killed in the war and would not return. We began to grow up.

One day, in early March of 1945, the doorbell rang just as we finished eating supper. Aunt Margaret opened the door to an Air Force officer and a pale gaunt woman who he introduced as Moira Walker. Major Smith identified himself and stated that he had orders to deliver this woman to our address and remain

*with her until she was in safe hands, at which time he
was to return directly to Moses Lake Army Air Base.*

*Aunt Margaret, while seeming calm, was shaken to
the core. We were all astounded when she made a
series of phone calls canceling her appointments for the
following day. She never did that. We knew it was
serious. It seemed like months but was probably only
about a week before Moira began to show signs of life.
We later learned that she had been injured while
attempting to prevent a former employer and German
spy, Harriet Malthorpe, from jumping in front of a
London bus.*

*From then on, Moira improved steadily. Soon after
Uncle Thomas returned to us in July, he and Moira told
us that they wanted Keiko and me to become their
daughters. We happily agreed and moved with them to
another house a few blocks away. The transition was
not difficult. We still felt that we were one family living
under two roofs. They told us that we could begin to
call them Mother and Father as soon as we were ready.
I don't think that took very long.*

*At war's end when a jubilant celebration took place
in downtown, no member of our family joined in the
festivities. Uncle Charles had been killed during one of
the last days of fighting in Europe. We kept "ourselves
to ourselves" as much as we could for a few weeks.*

*Eventually we resumed our regular routines and
grew into our adult selves. William, Bert, Catherine
and Keiko all live elsewhere and visit regularly. I,
Maemi, am the only one of the five of us who settled in
Spokane after attending Whitworth College. It was at
Whitworth where I met my husband Max Marshall. We
married immediately after graduating.*

*For many years I have had the privilege of sharing
thousands of cups of tea with Aunt Margaret and my
mother. I had learned much about them even before*

they produced the first box of letters that they had exchanged between England and Spokane from 1937 to 1945.

It was my father's spectacular accident that brought the letters to our attention. He had been an extremely active guy until he broke his left arm and his left leg in a dramatic and painful ice skating accident. He was not acting like his usual cheerful self; sitting around wearing heavy casts on two of his limbs did not suit him well. In fact, he became more cross with each day that he was trapped in his chair.

Finally, when my mother could stand his complaints no longer, she shoved the tin boxful of letters onto his lap and commanded: "See what you can do with these." Organizing these letters, writing a prologue and epilogue, and seeing them through the publication process gave my father pleasant work and kept his mind active through the rest of his recovery period. Published under the title Letters from Brackham Wood, the book has been read and enjoyed by many.

Many winters later, my father's disposition suffered once again as he began to experience new aches and pains. One morning he joked to my mother that he wished there was another set of letters to entertain his mind. Mother looked a bit shocked but did not reply. After talking with Aunt Margaret, she admitted that there was, indeed, another set of letters.

This correspondence had been written during the years that my mother and aunt were separated once again. I don't know if my father ever read them. Spring came and, feeling better as the warm weather returned, he resumed his regular routines. I did not see these letters again until quite recently when I was helping my mother clear out some of her old papers. Most of them were nestled in among a stack of tablecloths that had not been unfolded for years.

This second set of letters tells more about my Aunt Margaret, who was a "liberated professional" as well as a wife and mother before the term had been invented. They also describe post-war England and America and a nuclear power plant built in the middle of the state of Washington. But more dramatically they opened up a "can of worms" that led us to question my parents' involvement in international espionage.

* * * * *

September 4, 1947

My Dearest Margaret,

How very familiar and yet how strange it seems to be writing you once again from England. Familiar, because I wrote to you from here for seven years: strange, because the world and our lives have changed so drastically since last we exchanged letters. During the past two years in America I have put the war behind me. However, that war is very present again as I write from London, which still bears considerable wartime scars. Save that nothing is falling from the sky, it looks almost the same as it did when the war was raging.

The contrast between the clean and undamaged streets and buildings of Spokane and every other unbombed American town and the soot-coated, bomb-damaged city that I walked through today is almost impossible to describe. Much rebuilding has begun but the damage is evident on every street.

I know that our daughters are doing well under your care but I already miss them terribly. Leaving them with you was the most difficult thing I have ever done. They are very attached to your family and the home where they have lived for the past four years. The three girls have created a wonderful trio. Until Thomas and I get settled into our new routines, it is best not to move them.

We live in very nice rooms on the first floor of a semi-detached home in Highgate, which I will describe to you more thoroughly in another letter. Our postal address is 92 Talbot Road. I have not spent any time in the center of the city. I am still getting settled and need time to process my feelings.

We have been drinking the tea that you packed in my luggage. I think you predicted better than I what post-war England would be like. I had intended to share the tea with others but, since we could buy none until we received our coupons, we have been drinking much of it ourselves. Yesterday Thomas appeared with our ration books and this morning I was able to purchase a few basic food supplies on the High Street. We will eat at restaurants again today.

You will no doubt be surprised to hear that I am also working. It is not a full-time position but I am pleased to be helping. The exciting thing is that I have been given a Minox subminiature camera. Can you believe that it is three inches by about one inch and a bit over a half inch deep? I was shown how to use it by example and had no idea I had been photographed until my trainer revealed that he had taken six pictures of me as we talked.

Early this morning Thomas asked me if I would like to travel with him to Cambridge. Of course I replied that I would love to explore the town and university. I was taken aback when he made it clear that we could ride the train together and make light impersonal conversation as we travel but that I would need to leave the train and station on my own. Before we reached the Cambridge station, he gave me the hour to return and told me to board the next train for London whether or not I see him.

Tomorrow we will have some time to explore unless Thomas darts out again. I have done a bit of looking around the neighborhood and am anxious to show him what I have discovered. We live not far from Highgate Cemetery and I walked there for the first time yesterday. A famous novelist lies there. Under her pseudonym, George Eliot, is carved her birth name, "Mary Anne Cross." By all rights, she should be buried in Poets' Corner of Westminster Abbey but she was deemed ineligible for such an honor because she had denied the Christian faith during her lifetime.

The grave of Karl Marx is the most commonly visited gravestone in the cemetery. I was asked to use my Minox to snap pictures of his gravesite and to include any bystanders in the picture.

I shall have more news next letter, but I want you to have my address immediately so that we can once again be in contact. I miss you terribly.

Please tell the girls that I shall write notes to them tonight and post them on Monday. I have faith that our letters will travel faster than they did the last time we were separated.

anxiously await your return letter.

Much love,
Moira

September 29, 1947

Dearest Moira,

I am so glad to receive your letter and excited to finally have your address.

All of us are relieved to know that you and Thomas arrived safely and are now settled into your apartment on a street with a pleasant sounding name. I allowed the girls to read your letter. They were all smiles!!!

Your daughters are doing better than I would ever have expected! In fact, I think all the children believe this time to be just a giant slumber party. It took about five days for all of them to settle into a routine.

Maemi and Keiko miss you terribly, but are being very brave. I am aware of "letters in progress" from both girls to you. I suppose they must be writing every little thing that has happened to them since you and Thomas left. It was wise to leave the girls here as the school situation in London must be lacking teachers, classrooms and general organization.

Catherine made the transition to high school with ease. She doesn't seem fazed by the increase in homework. In fact, she is most anxious to complete it, especially on the day that she goes to *Dasidrian*. It is a drama club for high-schoolers city-wide. Her drama teacher is Alice Garvin Windsor. She is fantastic with the students. I know you were hoping to get the girls enrolled in classes with her before you left. Alice does have space for both girls and with your permission, I shall enroll them.

Bert is glad to finally be a high school senior and William just left for Chicago. The latter is very much looking forward to his second year at Northwestern. All of us went to the station to see him off!

Your house appears to be in good condition. The yard has been mowed, the fallen leaves have been raked and the renters have placed an autumn wreath on the door. When I have a moment, I will stop in to say hello, thereby being able to assess the interior.

After all those summer interviews, I finally hired a nanny, Julia Seginni Larson. She isn't "Mary Poppins," as Julia's temperament is a vast improvement on "Mary's," but she is magical and won the girls' hearts (Bert's and William's as well) when she created scalidi for them. Scalidi, I now know, are wonderful Italian confections made with eggs, sugar, flour and butter and then deep-fried. As a final touch they are dipped in honey. Yum!

Julia is 32 and widowed. She taught school for about four years in nearby Cheney, before returning to Whitworth to further her studies. She married in 1942, but lost her husband in the beginning days of the war. She has been living in her parents' home while looking for work. I hope what I am paying her will keep her with us. Perhaps the fact that she asked to do some private tutoring in our home, is an indication that she is satisfied with my arrangement. I thought her request was reasonable and readily agreed. Her small sitting room makes a perfect space to work with her students. At last, the house is back to running smoothly!

Sadly, Julia's only brother, John, returned from the South Pacific suffering from extreme combat exhaustion. He had flown with Pappy Boyington's squadron in 1944 over Rabaul, and was shot down and taken prisoner at the same time as Boyington. Both were eventually sent to a POW camp near Tokyo called Ōmori and were both liberated in August of 1945.

Pappy Boyington, a local boy of sorts, was born and lived in Coeur d'Alene and St. Maries, Idaho. He attended the University of Washington where he graduated with a degree in aeronautical engineering. After that, he worked at Boeing as a draftsman and engineer. What a small world! I wonder whether his path ever crossed my cousin Gillian's when she was at Boeing.

Julia says John appears listless and unkempt with almost mask-like facial expressions. He suffers from headaches, fatigue and chronic dysentery. He lives with his mother and father in the family home, but the situation is unsatisfactory and his parents are at their wits'end.

I suggested that she bring him to see the psychiatrist who recently joined the Montrose Clinic. I believe I told you about Dr. Ira Levinson. He and his wife escaped the Nazi Occupation of their native Austria by mere months. They came to the U. S. and settled in New York City.

Ira had already practiced for 10 years in Vienna, but it was necessary for him to go back to school to obtain his State Board certification and license. His wife, Erica, had a sister who lived in Spokane and when his schooling and licensure were completed, the Levinsons settled here to be near family.

You'll recall that the house east of ours is that of the Butterick family. Nancy, her husband George, their three children and two cats are wonderful neighbors. Nancy has gone to work selling "Stanley Home Products." It's a great way for women to earn money while still caring for their families. Nancy can sell her products when her children are in school or in the evenings when her husband is home with them.

What I have seen this past week is a different George from the one I thought I knew. When he got home from the war, George bought a refrigerated truck. I found it strange, but never inquired what he did with it.

I have a perfect view of the Butterick's garage's double barn doors from my kitchen window. On a couple of mornings last week, I had to be at the clinic early. The first morning I was up at five a.m. daydreaming at the kitchen table when I heard his truck arrive next door. As I watched, George opened the truck's back door and I could see the contents: large frozen pieces of beef!

That might not be odd except for the fact that Nancy told me that her husband worked for a tire company as the sales manager. A mystery on my street! I intend to pay more attention to the comings and goings of my neighbor.

I am beside myself with the news that you are employed again and have been charged with taking photos of subjects of whom you apparently don't ask permission. This sounds like a rerun of five years ago. We both know that ended disastrously. Why would you even think that this would end any differently? At the same time I am most curious to know why Thomas specifically asked you to take photos of people standing in front of Karl Marx's statue.

I am assuming that you are not telling me everything there is to tell about the subjects you catch on the lens of your Minox, but I am certainly more than a wee bit concerned that you are wandering around Highgate Cemetery and Cambridge on your own taking pictures with a camera the size of a compact. I would like to wring Thomas' neck! You have a family. The girls depend on you. They cannot suffer any more loss in their young lives.

I do want to assure you that all is well here. Try not to worry about your girls while you are at "work," though I know that is an impossibility!

With much love,
Margaret

October 15, 1947

Dearest Margaret,

Your letter came more quickly than I could have hoped. I am much relieved to hear that Maemi and Keiko are doing well and that Catherine is making the transition to high school so easily. I am deeply grateful that they came to your family at such an early age and that she has been such a wonderful big sister to them. Please do enroll them in Alice Garvin Windsor's drama classes. I myself dreamed of taking drama classes and am so pleased that they will be able to develop their talents.

Julia Seginni Larson sounds like a real jewel. I never doubted that you would find an excellent person to help you manage your busy life even though unattached women are "rare on the ground" just now. What a bonus that she has a teaching background. I imagine that concern about her brother encouraged her to accept your offer rather than to seek a full-time teaching position. She will be free to help her parents and John during the day if needed and still be able to tutor children who need help.

I am relieved to learn that our tenants are taking good care of our place. Do be careful watching your neighbor! I know full-well the dangers of curiosity. On the other hand, it is rather exciting to have a mystery going on right next-door!

Thomas and I were most fortunate to find lodgings in this ward where there is much less physical evidence of the recent war. He works long days from Monday through Friday while I enjoy some free time between the numerous daily tasks required to keep house in the England of today.

Maemi and Keiko both wrote that you are preparing a box to send to us, which will be most appreciated as I prepare meals. Shopping is the biggest task of my day. I stand in line at the bakery, the butcher shop, the dry goods store, the green grocer and the fishmonger as I did in the years before I came to the United States. Shortages continue and rationing is worse now than during the war. Each adult is allotted 13 ounces of meat, 8 ounces of sugar, 1 quart of milk and 1 egg per week. In restaurants, bread has become one of the three main courses. In other words, if we order bread, we forgo dessert.

Yesterday I waited for more than an hour to reach the front of the queue at the butcher shop only to find no gammon rashers in the case. The positive side of these interminable lines is the conversations I have with complete strangers. The practice of chatting with people I do not know, which I developed during the War, has been very helpful in becoming acquainted with neighbors.

I miss our daily chats very much. I am slowly learning about our landlady, Eileen Scott. Do you remember the tradition of "elevenses"? We have twice met at 11:00 to drink coffee and eat a digestive biscuit. We by no means talk as freely or laugh as much as you and I. However, it has been a pleasant way to become acquainted with one another. Miss Scott lived out my dream of becoming a teacher in a girls' school and retired after teaching maths for over 30 years at the Camden School for Girls. She left the school in 1939, shortly before the school was evacuated to Luton.

Eileen inherited this house in an amazing stroke of luck. After being hired to teach at the Camden School for Girls she took a room in the home of Miss Donna Kilgallen, an elderly spinster who had inherited it. Almost immediately after Eileen moved in, her landlady became very ill. Being a compassionate person, she took charge of Miss

Kilgallen's care both personally and by arranging for additional help.

Six years later, Miss Kilgallen passed away and Eileen was shocked but delighted to learn that she had inherited the house and the remainder of her landlady's fortune. She realized that she would not be able to run the home on her teacher's salary, and therefore, used her inheritance to renovate the house into flexible living space by adding two kitchenettes, two toilets and two bathrooms on the first floor and taking the ground floor as her own living space. We have the use of one kitchenette, toilet, bath, and two rooms; one we use as a bedroom and the other as a parlor.

Thomas sends his regards. I think that perhaps he is a bit homesick. He has been asking me many questions about Charles' military career. Specifically he wanted to know the date on his last letter and the particulars about how you received notification of his death. I find that I have very little memory of that time. I shall ask him to write his questions as they occur to him.

I will admit to having been a bit taken aback by your reaction to the news that I was once again doing a little work. After a moment's thought, however, I understood your reaction. To me, Thomas' request seemed the most natural thing in the world. I found myself falling easily into the role once I recovered from the shock of being told how to behave toward him.

As planned, we traveled to Cambridge last week in the same compartment but without really being together. We sat in companionable silence all the way. It was really rather fun. I pretended that I was an "extra" on a movie set.

I wore the tweed suit and coat that I had sewn nine years ago. The wind whipped up "a trouble" but I was quite comfortable in my overcoat, felt hat, and gloves. I kept my hands in my pockets most of the time as the newness of my gloves shone like a beacon. I noticed several people staring at them when I stopped to buy a biscuit. New leather gloves are just not worn by ordinary folk these days.

Exploring the streets of Cambridge was exhilarating. Cape-like robes flapped behind the dons and students alike as they rushed past me. With no agenda or purpose, I merely wandered. The bridges over the River Cam made me imagine that I was in Venice. I walked down a shopping street of half-timbered houses with overhanging upper stories. I saw the round medieval Church of the Sepulcher, first built in 1130 and King's College Chapel, which was begun during the reign of King Henry VI in 1446 and finished in 1515 when Henry VIII was on the throne.

I arrived at the station a full 40 minutes before 6:00, the return time that Thomas had given me, sat on a bench and began to read the "penny dreadful" that I had bought at a used bookstore. I paid no mind to the person who briefly sat next to me until I felt a slight nudge. By the time I turned my head, nothing was on the bench save an issue of *Woman* magazine. The cover portrayed a woman in elegant evening dress and the words, "simplest stitches make loveliest designs." I was amused because I was certain there was not a simple stitch anywhere on that dress. Then I noticed the first class train ticket tucked in between the pages like a bookmark.

Only then did I understand that Thomas had sat down, nudged me, and left the magazine without my catching a glimpse of him. The journey back was very pleasant. I saw that same man as he stepped into my compartment looking for something on the rack, and, not finding it, going on his way. I felt no rejection—only excitement.

I very much look forward to your next letter. By no means does a piece of paper replace our constant conversations. However, receiving your missives does a great deal to allay my anxiety about being away from home and family.

Much love,

Your cousin and sister
Moira

November 6, 1947

Dearest Moira,

There you see?! I knew that somehow you were going to be drawn into something nefarious, even if it just means a harmless "trial run" with your own husband! What in the world could Thomas have in mind for your future? I still can't believe that with two young girls waiting at home, you are willing to be doing something that could put either or both of you in harm's way. Perhaps you are just going to be a decoy to remove the interest from someone you don't even know, or perhaps deflecting attention from Thomas himself. I'm rather amused at the thought of you being an "extra" in a movie. I would certainly go to the movie just to see your expressions. I briefly wondered why you were wearing a suit and coat sewn nine years ago while reading the latest issue of *Woman*. It's now obvious to me that you were traveling incognito; maybe you are even trying to blend in with the population, rather than standing out in the crowd shouting, "I'm an

American." Truthfully, I am a bit jealous of the excitement you are experiencing! I can hardly wait for a description of your next adventure!

With regard to Thomas' questions about Charles: I found the telegram I received informing us of Charles' death. It was the same "we regret to inform you" message that so many received. I remember thinking: "How can this be? Hitler is dead. The war is over." The last time we had heard from Charles was a letter he had written Christmas, 1944. We didn't receive it until February, 1945. I recall saying that it was the best Valentine's Day present I had ever received. He didn't mention, of course, where he was or what he was doing. It was almost as if he weren't part of the war that had been raging. The telegram indicated otherwise: that he had died "from wounds inflicted in battle" on the morning of May 10, 1945. On June 1, 1945, we learned that Charles would never be coming home. I wonder why Thomas is pondering those horrible days.

I cannot believe that you have been gone nearly three months; it seems more like six! Time passes so quickly while I am at the clinic, but the weekends are so very long without you and Thomas.

The Three Musketeers are occupied with drama on Saturday morning, while Bert is at the Main Library all day. I'm glad that we live on the bus line! I have told the girls that they can stop at *The Crescent Fountain* for a soda before coming home, but most of the time they are eager to get home and complete their schoolwork so that Sunday is absolutely free. William is anxious for his finals the first week in December to be over. We all miss him terribly and are looking forward to his Christmas break.

Julia has begun to bake some Christmas cookies. We are allowed a taste, but most of the delights are going into tins for the holidays. She is a marvelous cook and we are very spoiled, not to mention, lucky to have her.

Her brother, John, has been admitted to Eastern Washington State Hospital in Medical Lake. I met him only once and that was the morning that Julia brought him to the clinic for his appointment with Dr. Levinson. I sat with them until they were called. John spent most of the time muttering something about Ft. Lawton in Seattle. Later when Julia and I were alone at home, I asked her about his obsession with the military post. She said that her brother had been stationed there when an Italian prisoner-of-war had been found hanged. Forty-four Negro soldiers were charged with a variety of counts, including riot and murder. Four of the defendants faced the death penalty. In the end, two soldiers had the charges against them dropped, 13 soldiers were acquitted, and 28 were convicted, two of manslaughter. She said her brother had nothing to do with the event, other than to have been stationed there at the time of the riot and the death. The hope is that with care and therapy, he will be able to reenter society. Perhaps, he saw something that drove him over the edge! At least, his parents can get some respite and Julia can relax... somewhat.

I have very sad news. Karen Blanchard passed away this past week. Larry is absolutely devastated at losing his wife as you can imagine. I suspect he will take time from work for several weeks. Karen was being treated with some experimental drugs with good results; although the drugs seemed to shrink the tumors, the results did not last long and she was returning every two or three weeks for another treatment. You might find the history of these drugs of interest.

The beginning of World War II caused great concerns over the possible use again of chemical warfare. The use of mustard gas during the Great War was so horrid. Interestingly, these concerns led to the discovery of nitrogen mustard as an effective treatment for cancer. Karen was treated with mustine, an agent related to mustard gas. She was also being treated with folic acid, which recently was found to be another effective cancer treatment. Poor Larry! He has cured many, but not this time. It was so difficult for him to stand by and watch Karen waste away. (I didn't mean to infer that he was treating his own wife; Jack Bailey was doing that. I think you know his wife, June, from the St. John's Guild.)

It's unbelievable that the English are still rationing! I have learned that a gift package from me to you, weighing more than 5 pounds, will be deducted from *your* rationing card! This is what we are going to do about that: In order to avoid going over the 5 pound maximum, I am sending several small packages. I wish I could send fresh fruits, but dried apples will have to do. You can also expect flour in two different packages, soda crackers, sardines, dried beef, and some parsley and mint seeds; at the very least you can grow an indoor herb garden!

I am amazed that so much money is being spent on Princess Elizabeth's wedding; it doesn't appear that the Royals are rationing!!! It is rather exciting that you are living in London. Perhaps you and your landlady, Eileen, will try to get a peek of her carriage and the festivities on the wedding day.

Speaking of Eileen…I do remember the tradition of "elevenses." In fact, I miss the days when you and I had time to stop for a chat, a scone and a cup of tea. Are you really drinking coffee with Eileen? How very American of both of you!

I am so happy that you have other women with whom to talk. It will make the time when Thomas is not at home go more quickly. You are missed by your

Guild friends. They frequently inquire about you. I gave them your address. Have you heard from any of them? Grace has been particularly interested to hear your news.

There is nothing new on George Butterick and the refrigerated truck. In fact, I haven't seen the truck for several days. Curiously, I have seen George coming and going, presumably to work…in a suit! I still believe that something untoward might be occurring next door. It makes me very sad. Nancy is a lovely woman and they have young children. During the war years, she worked so hard to keep her family going in George's absence. I hope he has not become involved in something criminal.

I am going to the Civic Theatre tomorrow night with the Levinsons. I feel like a third wheel, but at the same time I don't want to go alone. The production, *Blythe Spirit*, is at the Post Theater.

I haven't been out much in the evenings. I did take the children to see *Miracle on 34th Street*. At the very least it put us in the mood for Christmas, even though we saw it in October!!! The girls are beyond believing in Santa Claus, but still want to believe in his spirit.

I miss you so! It will be very strange to celebrate the holidays without you!

With love and regards to both you and Thomas,
Margaret

November 20, 1947

My Dear Margaret,
The devastating news in your letter has caused me to immediately put pen to paper. How I wish I could be with you at this difficult time. Karen

Blanchard will be much missed. I remember her well. She was such a kind lady and so supportive of Larry. The entire medical community must be heartbroken. Those in your profession dedicate themselves to keeping patients alive. I can only imagine the heartbreak when all resources fail, particularly for a loved one. I know that you will be of tremendous help to Larry. You have known each other for many years and have already been through a great deal together.

How astounding that medical treatment is being derived from agents of war! Imagine cures for cancer derived from substances designed to immobilize. This is hard to fathom, yet I suppose that we should be encouraged that good, such as treatment of cancer, can come from evil such as mustard gas.

I shall send a letter of condolence to Larry and write June Bailey as well. I became very fond of her as we worked together in the Guild and she recently sent me a lovely letter reporting on Guild activities and assuring me that I am missed. I hope to be back in time to help with some of the projects she described. Please send Grace my best wishes. She is a real spark and kept us all going with her wit and spirit.

I am not surprised that John Seginni is not well. The more stories I hear about the experience of war, the more I am grateful that more veterans do not experience severe difficulties upon returning home. I am certain that you contribute greatly to his recovery by pointing out resources that can facilitate his healing.

Thomas wants me to tell you that he is very thankful for the information you sent on Charles' death. At first he was devastated to learn that his brother made it through the entire war alive and then passed away two days after the end of hostilities in Europe. I have never seen my husband as upset as he was for the first few hours after he read your letter. I was relieved when he awakened the following morning with a renewed determination to uncover the truth.

Last week Eileen and I met with three other women over coffee. I heard stories of young men from this country who, like John, have been traumatized by their war experiences. We discussed a myriad of topics including wartime memories, the jubilation of V-Day, the return of soldiers and, of course, the shortages and rationing that plague these women daily as they try to feed and clothe themselves and their families while keeping their homes comfortable. They are also concerned about the lives their children will live in this post-war world.

To these topics I do not add much. It would only distress these women to learn of my comfortable post-war life in Spokane. The ease with which I washed clothes, the comfort of central heating, the convenience of hot water available at the turn of a tap, riding to the supermarket in a car, shopping for food only weekly, storing the perishables in my comparatively enormous American refrigerator, and the convenience of my electric range would only aggravate their misery. Nor would they enjoy hearing of the status that I was accorded simply by speaking with an English accent.

Last Sunday, Thomas and I took a walk through Highgate Wood, a pleasure that this difficult winter has denied us. We continued our walk for nearly a mile to get a look at Alexandra Palace. Known by its nickname Ally Pally, it was leased to the BBC in

1936 and has since served as its main transmitting center for television. The building, first constructed in 1873, was named for Princess Alexandra and it is rumored that the BBC transmitter was used for defense purposes during the war. The Ministry of Works is just now repairing the section of the "Pally" that was hit by a doodlebug during the war.

The BBC is transmitting once again and Thomas has promised to take me to a pub where one of those new "Teles" has been installed. I cannot imagine staring at such a box. I have seen moving images only on a screen in a theater. I have read that these boxes may eventually find their way into homes, which is hard for me to imagine. Where would such a device be placed in the average home? I imagine that it would require a very large space.

I am thrilled to hear that all five of our children are doing so well. Our girls could not be in better hands and I am happy for them. I thank you very much for assuring that they write us frequently. I cannot deny that being away from them is terribly painful. I very much look forward to our all being together very soon but I have no way of predicting when that will be.

Margaret, your perspicacity amazes me! How could you, from a distance of 6,000 miles, *possibly* know more about me than I know about myself? Indeed, a few days after my Cambridge adventure Thomas commented on how pleased he was at my behavior during that day. "My behavior?" I asked with perhaps a tinge of hostility in my tone. "How can you know absolutely anything about my behavior? You were nowhere near me." After a long and triumphant laugh, he admitted that he was indeed near me quite a bit and asked if I would enjoy exploring other places under the same conditions. Thomas looked pleased when I replied in the affirmative then left the room, quickly returning carrying a fair number of boxes.

After forewarning me that his next statement was a compliment, he explained that he had been observing me closely and discovered that I disappeared easily into crowds. In fact he had become concerned when he entered the station to set the magazine with ticket beside me on the bench. He then scanned the benches carefully and watched every entrance and exit. I was puzzled to hear this because, as you may remember, I arrived there 40 minutes early. He then confessed that, during his fifth scan of the territory, he realized that I had been sitting there all along. I had been invisible! Can being invisible be such a good thing? I teased him that it might just have been the "penny dreadful" I was reading that put him off the scent.

He then handed me the boxes one by one. In the order he presented them they contained: three felt hats, each of a slightly different design but the same vintage as the one I wore in Cambridge, two pairs of spectacles with plain glass lenses, and one beautiful, beautiful evening dress with all accessories including jewelry and shoes. He explained only this one. In the future we will be attending a party with some of his colleagues.

Thomas has been spending a great deal of time with a man who has recently come to London to work at the Russian Embassy and who has many questions about the customs and ways of thinking of both the British and the Americans. Yuri asked around until he heard of an American journalist who displayed very little of the "typical American bombast" and who was married to a woman who had grown up in England. Yuri made arrangements to meet Thomas.

Thomas has introduced him to several important people, including the editor of *The Times*. He also arranged to take Yuri to the inner sanctum of the *Athenaeum*, one of the most exclusive of the Gentlemen's Clubs in London. I confess that I have no idea how Thomas gained access to this establishment whose first secretary was Michael Faraday, and that boasts William Makepeace Thackeray, Charles Dickens and many Nobel Laureates among its former and current members.

Before I close this lengthy letter, I must tell you that Thomas and I are both grateful for your continued supply of parcels. They make life so much easier and receiving them in packages weighing under five pounds each makes it seem like Christmas is already here. I cannot imagine what Christmas will be like without the girls and with no knowledge of when I will see them again. You will all be missed terribly.

I am so very pleased that our letters travel so much faster than they did during the war.

I cannot express in words my gratitude for all you do and have done for us.

Much love,
Moira

December 11, 1947

Dearest Moira,

As always, I was delighted to hear from you. I am not surprised that you have gone to work, but it most certainly surprises me that your "work" will involve a disguise or multiple disguises! I was hoping that your talents would be used at a desk...but when you mentioned a camera, warning bells began to ring...loudly!

"You disappear easily in crowds?" I think that must be a compliment...referring to your cat and mouse abilities! I have a sense, however, that danger lurks in those crowds; even more danger than your near brush with death trying to save Harriet in 1945. I can only assume that Thomas has returned to his "former work." You don't say for whom *you* are working. The chills that run up and down my spine tell me that you are involved with whomever Thomas is. Just who is that?!

I know why you waited to get to the end of your letter before telling me about Yuri, a Russian no less! You undoubtedly knew that I would hit the roof! Doesn't it give you pause to think that this Yuri character "asked around until he heard of an American journalist who displayed very little of the 'typical American bombast' and who was married to a woman who had grown up in England?" It sounds to me like Yuri was looking for someone who met specific qualifications. Don't you find it at all curious that the two of you meet those requirements perfectly? If I were a gambler I would wager that Thomas knew about Yuri all along and has now succeeded in situating Yuri exactly where *he* wants Yuri to be. It does not surprise me that Thomas has ways and resources to enter any establishment in London that he chooses; what does surprise me is that it is with a Russian in tow. In what have you become embroiled?

In the dull world of Spokane this is what is happening: William arrived home last week just in time to go on the annual Christmas tree trek. We went this past weekend to the cottage for an overnight. It took several hours before the place was warm enough to remove our extra layers, but that didn't seem to matter to any of us.

It was a joy to watch our children romping in the snow looking forever like very young children instead of teens. We ate chili and cornbread for dinner and returned home the next day with a beautiful fir. It now stands in the living room in all its glory!

Your girls remain strong and, thankfully, healthy in your absence. However, the approach of Christmas without their parents is obviously affecting them. If it were only possible to find suitable schooling for them, they would so benefit from time not only with you and Thomas, but also the learning experience itself. Do not let my musings worry you; Catherine is playing "Mother Hen" to both of the girls. They have become like three peas in a pod.

Bert has been given an additional task at the Library. He was asked to read excerpts from Betty MacDonald's recently published book, *Mrs. Piggle Wiggle*. He read to parents and children during the Saturday Children's Hour at Main Branch of the Public Library. He was very excited to do this, shades of his childhood days of reading to my friends' children.

What really excites him (all of us, actually) is that Spokane recently received a gift of land west of the city from the John Aylard Finch estate. Currently, parts of the land contain housing previously leased to the military for use during the war. Once the housing, or part of it at least, is removed, the city can begin to develop not just another park, but an actual arboretum! Everything that deals with nature excites Bert. I think most Spokanites are excited, too. I can only imagine how lovely it will be to stroll through the arboretum on a sunny fall afternoon, not to mention the learning that will be enhanced by all the varietals that can be planted.

Have you been able to see any of your friends from Brackham Wood? A letter, postmarked from your former home, came last week. It has no return address so I do not know from whom it came. I am sending it on to you in a different mailing.

With Larry still reeling from Karen's loss, I went in his place to Seattle to confer with Group Health Cooperative of Puget Sound doctors regarding their practice model. Group Health purchased a medical clinic, which had its own small hospital and began a member-governed practice which affords prepaid medical coverage to people who otherwise would not have it. They already have 8,500 members enrolled in their plan. That is amazing considering they organized just 10 months ago! The plan is not without problems, however. One huge obstacle is that King County Medical Society opposes *group* practices. They support only solo practices. As a result, some hospitals refuse staff privileges to the Group Health Physicians. Who knows what the future may bring to our clinic?

I rather liked being on my own in an official capacity. Since the war ended, women seem to have once again been relegated to the back seat. The only down-side was being away from the children. Julia managed things well, so I am confident that I can be gone without worry…for a brief time, that is.

Do be careful in involving yourself in dangerous situations. I know that you must be able to recognize what things can go wrong. You have two girls who depend on your continued presence in their lives. They would not be able to tolerate your loss, nor the loss of Thomas. We, too, depend on you—both of you—remaining in our lives for a very long time. I cannot fathom losing you again, Moira.

I have no experience in your "business." However, I hope that the disguise that Thomas has provided you in no way resembles what you wear when you are Moira Edwards Walker. Put that 10-year-old coat in the rummage bin; it may look too much like the clothing Thomas has provided you. Or at the very least, only wear it as part of your disguise! Please purchase some up-to-date garments like those in the latest issue of *Woman* and wear those, not the clothes Thomas has chosen for you or even the clothes that you brought to London when you are portraying yourself. Your very life may depend on looking totally unlike the wife of Thomas Walker when you are weaving in and out of shops or whatever other god-forsaken place Thomas sends you.

With love and hope for your continued safety and good health,

Margaret

P.S. I am really just a bit envious of you. Getting to skulk around in disguise is just too much like a plot of a mystery book. We need to keep our letters, so that in our dotage we can remember just how "modern" and "daring" you were!

December 29, 1947

Dear Margaret,
The pull to be in Spokane with you for Christmas was painful. We missed each and every one of you. I can smell that hand-cut fir tree as if I were sitting in your living room and was very emotional at the prospect of being away for the holiday.

I am so pleased that you were able to get away on your own in a professional capacity. No doubt you, like I, were shocked to be away from our combined

family life as you travelled to Seattle alone. Coming here was the hardest transition of my life. When I was a maid-of-all-work I moved easily from household to household. Leaving loved ones is an entirely different matter.

Thank you for your perspective on Thomas' activities. I tend to agree with you. Perhaps he and Yuri are engaged in a mutually beneficial arrangement.

Thomas knows of, and keeps a key to, the undamaged flat of a friend who is away so we took the opportunity to stay in central London from Thursday through today. During that time we walked and walked as we explored different parts of the city. Thomas talked with people on the street and I was reminded of the embarrassment I had felt when, shortly after we met, he struck up a conversation with a total stranger; something just not done on the streets of London. My embarrassment turned to surprise when he was answered in a friendly manner. His American accent was the signal that class distinctions could be ignored.

Even though much destruction is still in evidence, the city bristles with vibrant activity. People walk the streets with energy and manage to dress smartly even while wearing clothing that shows its age. Skirts have been shortened and cuffs removed to eliminate frayed hems and sleeves. Shoes and handbags are kept polished to disguise wear. Missing buildings are still much in evidence, though the rubble has been removed. Some are being used as ersatz playgrounds by neighborhood children.

I shared your clothing advice with Thomas and we went about constructing an appropriate wardrobe to wear in my everyday life. We found two fashionable dresses with just a bit of wear and one brand new dress to supplement the wardrobe that I brought from Spokane. However, rather than giving away my ten-year-old clothing, we brought it to this London flat. He tells me that the old wardrobe will help me "put on invisibility." I have had a little practice while here and find it rather fun to meld in with the crowd, which is certainly no difficult task in one of the world's largest cities.

We are about to lock up this London flat and travel back to Highgate. I shall finish this letter after we arrive.

Back at Talbot Road

Eileen greeted us at the door in a state of great consternation or, as we say here "all of a do dah." She had received news that her sister, Eleanor, who lives in York, had just been taken to hospital and been through an extensive emergency surgery. When she is released, she will need help for at least six months. Eileen wants very much to be there. She has neither the time nor the inclination to find someone to stay in her part of this house while she is away and has offered us the full use of her home if we pay the gas and electricity bills and tend the garden.

She had given this much thought and had anticipated my first objection, which was, of course, that I could not be away from the girls for that long. She offered to intercede for us to get Maemi and Keiko admitted to the nearby Camden School for Girls where she taught maths for many years before she retired. From what she knows of them, she is certain that it would be a very good fit. It has a well-developed drama program as well as excellent academics. She is also certain that she could arrange for them to be admitted to winter term even if they enroll late. Of course, they would be day students.

Could this happen? Would it be good for them? If you think it possible, Thomas is willing to fly to New York, and take the train to Chicago, where he can do some business and then accompany them across the Atlantic either by ship or on one of the new transatlantic flights.

I am "all of a twitter" at the possibility. Dear cousin, please reply quickly. I am positive that you will know the right thing to do.

With much love to you and Maemi and Keiko and William and Bert and Catherine,

Moira

P.S. The letter postmarked Brackham Wood sits unopened beside me, having been delivered in my absence. I shall read it directly after I return from the Post Box. I anxiously await your return letter.

January 16, 1948

Dearest Moira,

Since you chose not to answer some of my queries, I can only assume they were questions to which you cannot respond. And if my assumption is correct, it tells me that you must be working on something of which you can only speak in generalities, or not at all. Therefore, I shall try not to dig too deeply into exactly what it is that Thomas has you doing. However, I will definitely be "reading between the lines" and therefore have only myself to blame for foolish conjectures.

So you have updated and added to your wardrobe. I imagine you had a wonderful time shopping; a lovely diversion to take your mind off craters, bombs and troubles the English people are having. We are so fortunate not to have had war on our shores! As for leaving some of your clothes in an "unoccupied for the moment" flat, I shall just have to imagine when and where you'll be wearing them. I now leave this topic with the only thing I know is safe to say, "Do be careful!"

The chastising over; I want to say I am thrilled for you and Thomas! The prospect of being reunited with your girls is absolutely wonderful. Of course, we will *make* it happen! Thomas' work must be very flexible to be able to leave London in a moment's notice, but I am very glad it is so. The following is what I propose:

I am planning to attend an AMA meeting in Chicago February 5-8. I can take your girls with me using my pass on the "Empire Builder" on Sunday, February 1. It will take us about 30 hours to get to Chicago, where we will await Thomas' arrival at the Drake Hotel. We'll be in a Pullman car the entire distance which will keep all of us rested. Air travel is too "iffy" in the winter and I for one need my sleep. Additionally, the fare is nothing to speak of by using my railroad pass. Thomas can meet us at the hotel and make the rest of the journey back to you whenever and by whatever means you have decided based on his schedule.

I will complete my reservations for the meeting and will do the same for the train for both myself and for Maemi and Keiko. No money needs to be spent until we get to Chicago, so should your plans change, no money will have been exchanged. All you need to do is send me Thomas' plans. Perhaps considering the time constraints, a telegram would ensure that I receive the information with room to spare. By the way, there is no difficulty in canceling the girls' reservations. Julia will be here anyway to care for Bert and Catherine, and the girls should you change your minds.

Our girls are going to be in the *Dasidrian Winter Program* in a couple of weeks. Each girl is to do a reading of her own choosing and must use a hat or some sort of visual addition.

The older students, Catherine included, will present a one-act play following the individual performances. Maemi has chosen (with a bit of help from me) a poem entitled, *The Pirate Don Durk of Dowdee.* She looks wonderful in Bert's pirate hat and he helped her create a mustache which I hope remains in place during the recitation! At the moment I cannot think of what Keiko has chosen, but it is about trees. Julia has helped her make a hat covered with felt leaves of fall colors and she is wearing a brown dress.

About the holidays: I'm certain they were difficult for you and Thomas, but I hope you are enjoying Steinbeck's, *The Pearl.* Maybe you'll recall that it was first published in *The Ladies' Home Companion* under the title, *The Pearl of the World.* The movie, which is also called *The Pearl,* is due to be in the theaters sometime this year. I read that Steinbeck insisted that the movie be made by a Mexican film crew with Mexican actors; that is a first!

I have worn the tam you sent several times already. Thank you so much! It snowed heavily last week, causing multiple accidents each time. But it created a beautiful snow world. I wear it each time it snows heavily thinking that should I become lost in the blizzard, someone would surely find me because of the tam's bright colors!

The children sledded or skated daily at Manito Park during Christmas vacation. We didn't try to get to the cottage as there was so much snow. On New Year's Eve, we had a hot chocolate party after a late afternoon skate. The girls each invited a friend to spend the night, while Bert had four of his buddies here, just briefly, as they had another invitation for the remainder of the evening.

I invited Larry, the Levinsons, and a nurse, whom we recently hired, and her husband. You'll never guess who the nurse is! Sarah Feingold, now Sarah Jacobs! I will tell you more about her in my next letter as the story is lengthy!

The adults came about 7:00 after the children had gone upstairs to giggle. Julia made a wonderful dish for us called Braciole. She used thin slices of beef which she had covered with a mixture of spinach, cheese, onions, mushrooms and lots of garlic and then wrapped the beef around itself and secured it with toothpicks. She then cooked the bundles in a tomato sauce. Delicious! Happy New Year!

Once all were back in school, I had a couple of difficult days. I feel Bert slipping away, just as William did two years ago. Soon both will be in college and then suddenly they will both be gone! The joy of seeing them grow into young men cannot be put into words. Charles would be so proud of them!

I wonder sometimes what life would be like had Charles survived the war. I do know that he would not have been pleased with President Truman's assessment of the Spokane newspaper as being one of the "two worst newspapers in the country!" The other paper he says is the *Chicago Times*. Of course, Truman would like neither as both are staunchly Republican. I can only imagine that our lives would have been much the same as mine is now; the only difference is that we would be able to share our pride in our children and we could grow old together.

I do have a bit of cheery news to share before I hurry my letter to the post office. I have been elected to be secretary of the State Medical Society…finally there is a woman on the Board!

It is all rather exciting and I do intend to make my presence known. In fact next week, I am going with the Society's president to Benton County to meet with the local Society in Richland. I doubt that I will get a peek at the Hanford Project, but I'm told that the growth of that area of the state is unbelievable and practically bursting at the seams with the influx of workers at Hanford.

It's still very hush, hush and frankly no one really knows what is going on out in the desert, other than that the proudest boast of the Hanford management is: "the complete success of safeguards against radiation injuries" and that the "Health Divisions of Hanford conduct research on the effect of radiation on living tissue." My comment on that is that the public's growing fear of radiation has caused the American Medical Association to develop a list of physicists deemed to be qualified to calibrate x-ray machines. So one has to wonder whether the "research" that is going on at Hanford is enough to protect the burgeoning population outside the "secure" area of the Project.

On that note, I will close. You both are loved and missed! I do hope we can make this plan work and that you can soon be together as a family!

Love,
Margaret

January 31, 1948

My Dear Margaret,

Happy New Year!!

It will be a great year now that I know that the girls will be with us soon. Their arrival becomes more real with each passing day. Now that the details have been ironed out between us in a flurry of telegraph messages, we have begun preparing for the girls' arrival by reorganizing Eileen's house for our larger family and making provisions for their education.

True to her word, Eileen secured a placement for them in the Camden School for Girls. We are confident that they will do well though it will no doubt be a bit of an adjustment. We shall enroll them as soon as possible. From the tone of their letters I fear they expect London to be much more like Spokane than it truly is. They will no doubt be shocked, as was I when I arrived here, by the sight of bombed out ruins. I could be wrong, however. They may see it all as a big adventure. Destruction here in Highgate is less evident than in the center of the city, though I have learned that at least seven bombs fell on or very near our own Talbot Road during the Blitz.

Thank you so much for the wonderful Christmas gift. You always know just what to send. Thomas and I have both read the book and enjoy talking about its themes. Surrounded by constant reminders of the destruction of war, the themes of greed, materialism, and what is worthwhile are comforting to read.

The bright red tartan tam certainly will signal rescuers should you be caught in a snowstorm and buried to the shoulders. I do miss the beautiful Spokane snowfalls of the past two winters with their muffled sounds and the peace they bring. This seems an especially damp and grey winter here.

Heartiest congratulations on being elected to the position of secretary of the State Medical Society. A woman on the Board will be a great asset to the Society and I know the organization will benefit mightily from having you in a position of leadership. You are not only a woman but a very knowledgeable, organized and competent physician. Having you aboard will benefit and raise the standard of the officers.

I am so pleased that you will be able to attend the national meeting of the medical profession. You have not done that for many years and it will, no doubt, inspire you as you move into the next stage of your career. I shall report to you as the National Health Service takes hold in this country. I cannot imagine that the transition will be smooth but shall watch it with great interest. Since our fathers served as small town doctors at one time, we should have a good perspective on the changes in both countries.

How interesting that you will be near the secret Hanford Project. Of course, we hear nothing of it on this side of the Atlantic. Their boast of "no radiation problems" indicates to me that something is amiss.

The letter you forwarded to me from Brackham Wood was from Patricia Dimblebey, the wife of Vicar Vincent Dimblebey, and was choc-a-block with information about the villagers and their current activities.

George Malthorpe is still in town and remains the proprietor of his haberdashery. Unbelievably, Patricia tells me that no one in the village has inquired after Harriet. Some things are just not discussed (at least with the vicar's wife) in an English village. However, should he volunteer any information, I am sure people within miles would hear it within the hour. What a contrast to our

Spokane neighborhood where he would have been thoroughly questioned the moment her absence was noticed. If he did not suppress the speculation with a clear answer, speculation would have run rampant until some piece of it became accepted as fact.

I was very glad that you wrote of Charles in your last letter. Your new career commitments and the growing independence of your children will open up a new life to you. Charles would be so proud of how bravely you have continued on and of the progress of your children. Since you have mentioned him, I feel that I can now tell you of some of Thomas' activities which I did not mention for fear of opening up old wounds. Thomas is absolutely determined to discover what happened to his younger brother during the war. He is troubled by the large gap in time between your last letter from Charles and the time that you were notified of his death. He will not rest until he uncovers the truth.

New Year's Eve with hot chocolate and a houseful of children and young adults must have been glorious. I am fairly bursting to tell you of the New Year's Eve Party we attended. You might find it strange, as did I, that we once again spent the night in the friend of Thomas' flat in central London when our home is a mere half hour tube ride away. I surmise that the "friend" is not often here, judging by his perfectly furnished and equipped flat that holds no hint as to the character of its owner. The only personal items in the entire flat are my two suits, a couple of plain frocks, my coat and few of my accessories, all of which are kept locked in the wardrobe.

I brought with me the beautiful black dress that I mentioned in my November letter. It has a pierced fabric top in the design of thick lace inserted into what otherwise would be a V-neckline. Two hours before the event was to begin, Thomas told me that two women were coming to dress me for the party. They arrived only moments after the words, "Whatever do you mean they are coming to dress me?" left my mouth. I was then scrubbed, buffed, sanded, powdered, rouged, curled, pulled and lacquered. Special undergarments provided whatever my own body did not.

When the two had finished with me, I looked into the mirror to face a complete stranger. How did I feel? I felt a little like a trussed-up pig and a little like a geisha who had forfeited the many years of required training and practice.

A different feeling entirely came over me as we entered the ballroom and all eyes fell on us. Under my heavy makeup I was blushing scarlet red but perhaps I enjoyed the recognition just a bit. I felt like Cinderella at the Ball as Thomas steered me through the crowd, stopping to introduce me to many people.

As we moved about the room, I caught a glimpse of Malcolm Blake, the brother of Harriet. You will remember that it was the shock of witnessing Harriet's violent death that propelled me across the ocean and landed me on your doorstep in a state of shock. Malcolm and I had celebrated several Christmas holidays together during the years that I was a maid in his sister's home. It was he, in fact, who had insisted that I be included in the family festivities.

After seating me behind a large potted plant, Thomas steered Malcolm over to a chair at our table and said: "You remember my wife, Moira." The poor man needed that chair. He looked completely shocked. He had not recognized me. Thomas and I both had a clear memory of a strikingly similar reaction five years ago, on New Year's Eve of 1943 when Thomas attempted to introduce us. Malcolm had replied that he had known Moira Edwards for over seven years and this certainly was not Moira. Perhaps Malcolm possesses poor facial recognition or perhaps I am a chameleon.

While my work as a maid had given me considerable practice at being invisible, absolutely nothing I had ever done prepared me for the type of recognition I received at this party. I thought about Eliza Doolittle, a character in the play *Pygmalion* written by George Bernard Shaw. She had been transformed from a flower seller at Covent Garden to a princess. I fell into bed that night completely exhausted.

I doubt that I will ever enter that same flat again. I have been informed that if I should need access to my working wardrobe in the future I will be given its location shortly before my next assignment begins. Maemi and Keiko's arrival will bring me new responsibilities and perhaps my life will become more predictable. I am so anxious to see them that I can scarcely contain myself.

Is there a chance you, William, Bert and Catherine could visit us here? We can provide comfortable accommodation. An international experience would be wonderful for you at this stage of your lives. We could even take our children to visit our childhood homes. No need to answer now, but keep it in mind. Perhaps the medical community will finance your trip in exchange for a report on our transition to The National Health Service.

With love to you all,
Moira

February 16, 1948

Dearest Moira,

WOW! The New Year's Eve Party sounded exhilarating, nerve-wracking and enchanting all rolled into one.

I have visions of you as a Lauren Bacall look-alike. The intrigue. The mysterious Mrs. Walker. The disguise. It's like a scene from a movie. I wonder whether you will be "dressed" every time you go out with Thomas to official events. I hope I have this correct: when you are Mrs. Thomas Walker, you are dressed to the nines; the glamorous Moira. When you are the matron with the Minox, you are dressed in British customary. I am relieved to know that you can carry off the disguise and the personality switches. It undoubtedly makes you safer! I suppose it is best to have a different flat from which you operate the charade. It would be so dangerous to have someone follow you back to the flat where you and your family are actually in residence.

I can only imagine your joy when you met Thomas and the girls at Heathrow. They were probably exhausted after the long 16-hour flight; but then the Lockheed Constellation has reclining seats, so perhaps not. I recall that the flight plan was from New York City to Gander, Newfoundland, on to Shannon Airport in Ireland and finally to Heathrow. What an unbelievable experience for your daughters! I can hardly wait to hear their tales of air travel. You, undoubtedly had a warm cozy room decorated in chintz, if you could find it, prepared for the girls and a delicious meal as well.

Indeed, the life ahead for the girls will be an adjustment, but they are young and bright but most importantly are back in the arms of their parents. They have met so many challenges already in their young lives. I should think this will be nothing to them!

I am so grateful to Thomas for his persistence in resolving the question of Charles' death. All of us, I dare say, would like to know what *really* happened. It is impossible to close that chapter until we finally have a definitive answer. I doubt that could come in any form other than Thomas finding the truth. I sometimes wonder if that is really Charles in the grave at Fairmont. It's ghoulish really, but what if it isn't?

My AMA meeting in Chicago was very productive and informative. However, it was very strange to be among so many men without Charles. I don't know why I say that as the meetings never included him, but dinner was different... a bit uncomfortable the first evening. How I managed to be seated with seven others I had never met, I will never know, but by evening's end it was as if we had always known one another. There were three couples and Dr. William (Bill) Morgan, a plastic surgeon from Boston, and myself. I suspect Bill is about 10 years older than I. Currently, he is a professor at Harvard where he teaches in the 10-year-old Maxillofacial Program. During the war years, he served as an Army medical officer. I can't recall where he was stationed but he worked primarily on facial repair. Coincidently, for a few weeks near the end of the war, he was at Baxter General here in Spokane, but that was after I had already left. He and I had dinner together a couple of evenings later in the week. Since 1948 is a Leap Year, maybe this is my year to find a mate! Could I really propose to someone?

One very odd thing happened on the return from the meeting. The second day out, I was seated in the dining car waiting for my breakfast to be served when I noticed a man sitting at the next table facing me. He looked very familiar. I didn't want to stare or draw attention to the fact that I was actually doing just that. I did make eye-contact with him once but, he did not react in any manner that led me to believe that he knew me. The encounter bothered me the entire trip. I didn't see him again until we got to Spokane, where much to my surprise, he too, got off the train. By the time I was in the station, he had disappeared. He had been dressed in heavy clothing; like a lumber-jack would wear. He had a large mustache and wore glasses. In spite of the glasses, I could see that he had the most unusual green eyes. I think that was what I found familiar.

The next day as I was driving out of my driveway, I saw George Butterick going into his garage. He turned and waved...no mustache, no lumberjack clothing, but those most unusual green eyes; definitely he was the man on the train. I can't fathom why he was dressed and disguised the way he was. He is supposedly a tire salesman!

Back to the real world. Larry has returned to work; it's a struggle, but the practice is very busy, which helps.

The house is very quiet without your girls. Catherine goes about her activities, but I know she misses them; Bert does as well. I am pondering a move to a smaller house. I really don't want to get involved with new construction, but in a way, it might be the best way to start over. All the children will be gone in a couple of years...I don't want to become an old woman rattling around in this house alone!

Life seems almost as if the war had never occurred! The economy is active, construction is up and new products seem to appear overnight! I don't know what I did before I had hair spray; do you have it yet? And then there is that wonderful Tupperware! A plastic container and lid in a variety of shapes serves as a way to preserve left-overs without spoilage. New mothers are demanding disposable diapers! I bet some inventor is working on that at this very moment!

Speaking of new products, I must tell you that, as of late, my vision has seemed strained. After an appointment with the ophthalmologist, I discovered that I needed glasses.

Choosing a frame is difficult when your eyes have been dilated. (I wish you had been here to help me!) Try to imagine this: the "browline" frames I chose are constructed so that the upper portion of the frame is thicker than the lower portion. The upper part, the "brows" and the "temples," are light tortoise-shell plastic and the lower part including the bridge is made of thin-rimmed wire which is held in place in the brows with little screws. I recently saw Sarah Feingold Jacobs and her husband, Lloyd, who I learned is one of the three Emergency Room doctors at Sacred Heart Hospital. They scarcely recognized me with my new spectacles.

I must digress here for a moment. You undoubtedly recall the many times I had to, in the middle of the night, attend an emergency. Now that ERs are staffed with physicians like Lloyd, house calls are becoming a thing of the past. Emergency patients are now seen 24 hours a day at the hospital. The ER doctor then reports, the following day, to the patient's doctor. If the patient requires hospitalization, it can be done immediately; if not, the ER doctor merely treats the patient and sends him home.

What I started to say in my last letter, was that both Sarah and Lloyd, are carefully watching, as all of us are, the situation in Palestine. They actually want to move to Israel! Last May, the United Nations resolved that, "a committee prepare for consideration at the next General Assembly, the question of Palestine." Their report proposed a plan to replace the British Mandate with "an independent Arab State, an independent Jewish State, and the city of Jerusalem," *all* to be under an International trusteeship which the General Assembly essentially adopted last November. Then, in December, bands of Arabs began attacking Jewish targets. I cannot believe that Sarah and Lloyd are considering moving there in the middle of the strife!

It would be a dream to come to visit you! But I'm afraid that it would be virtually impossible at this time as we four are going in different directions all the time. Catherine and I might be able to work something out for a summer vacation visit, but the boys need to work and could not afford to take time from their jobs. It is a lovely idea and I do thank you.

I look forward to hearing of the girls' progress and of how wonderful it is to have them back with you!

Love,

Margaret

March 12, 1948

My Dear Margaret,

How can I ever thank you for all that you did to make the best possible arrangements for our little girls? And they did look like very little girls indeed as they deplaned at Heathrow. It seemed like an eternity until all four propellers stopped revolving and the door was opened. The girls were very drowsy. I half dragged, half carried Keiko into the airport building while Thomas did the same for Maemi.

Thomas reports that the girls had been so excited for the first five hours of the flight between Gander, Newfoundland, and Shannon, Ireland, that they visited with every one of the other 50 passengers on

board. It turned out to be unfortunate for Thomas that one woman, a Mrs. White, told Keiko that, on an earlier flight, her friend was seated on the toilet when a pressure valve failed, turning her into a human cork between the pressurized cabin and the unpressurized waste tank. In order to free her, the pilot was forced to decrease the altitude of the aircraft and depressurize the cabin. I say it was unfortunate because for the rest of the flight both girls insisted that Thomas stand directly outside the toilet room door whenever either one of them were inside. The way he told the story caused me to burst out in raucous laughter. I still grin when I think about it.

It took only minutes for our luggage to arrive in the prefabricated Royal Air Force hut that currently serves as the terminal for Heathrow Airport. Only months ago an Army tent served that purpose. Our family ride to London was a complete pleasure for me. My family was together again. However, the girls were much affected by the destruction they saw on both sides as we made the journey to Highgate.

The amount of luggage they brought with them was both staggering and welcome. I marveled as I unpacked. The food, fabric, thread and the other surprises you sent should keep us in good supply for some weeks, perhaps months. We do appreciate you and all the thought that went into your packages.

The girls have settled into the house nicely. However, one morning I heard Maemi call out for Catherine as she was getting dressed.

We wish you could visit soon but understand completely why you cannot come but perhaps one day when this is all over and we are in our dotage we shall travel together to England.

I am not surprised but very happy to hear that your AMA meeting in Chicago was a great success. It must be years since you were away from home for so long. Dr. William Morgan from Harvard? I anxiously await further description. His having spent time in Spokane no doubt must have given you much fodder for conversation. He must be quite attractive if you are already writing me about popping the question.

Another part of your letter concerns me very much. I worry about the green-eyed man's appearance in two guises: lumberjack and tire salesman. I believe that you have written of him before. Neither a lumberjack nor a tire salesman should need a refrigerated truck. Keep a wary eye on him.

Thomas insists that I write and tell you that it would be normal for you to recognize him in your neighborhood but he advises you to not acknowledge him in other settings. Should he be traveling in disguise, he will be alerted if you give him more than a cursory glance. Please keep your eyes open and be careful. Thomas asks me to warn you not to look surprised or show in any way that you recognize him when you see him in disguise.

So you now have new fashionable glasses. I can't wait to see them and am pleased that you no longer suffer from eyestrain but I am surprised that Sarah did not recognize you. They must indeed be striking pieces of eyewear because she has known you for a long time. I enjoyed her company and am glad that she is now happily married to an emergency room doctor. I will hold positive thoughts for them but must admit that the thought of them moving to an unstable part of the world frightens me.

I wonder what our fathers would think of the concept of an emergency center. As English country doctors they were called out more nights than they were home. Medicine here remains much as it was then.

Thomas continues to work on his search for wartime information about Charles. He has heard of a chaplain who might be able to help but has not yet been able to connect with him. Knowing his dogged determination, I am quite certain that he will eventually find a satisfactory answer to all of our questions.

Watching Maemi and Keiko acclimatize themselves to their new surroundings is quite entertaining. I was amused and delighted by their reaction to the old geyser mounted over the bathtub taps. You and I both grew up without hot water taps. Taking our weekly baths required our mothers to heat the water on the kitchen stove, pour it into a tub on the kitchen floor and add enough cold water to prevent us from scalding ourselves. Since you and I are both an only child we always bathed in clean water. In larger families the children were bathed in order of cleanliness. The dirtiest family members, who were nearly always boys, were last. My father told me that he was never completely clean until he became an adult.

The only real challenge now is switching the geyser on early enough, (the large one in this house takes two hours to heat), remembering to switch it off before it explodes and, of course, adding the right amount of cold water.

The girls have made a fast friend of Anna Bradbury, a girl who also recently moved into the neighborhood and lives just down the road. As luck would have it she has enrolled in the Camden School for Girls. She has a brother, Ian, who is currently living with other relatives. Anna and her mother Sylvia live with Sylvia's sister, Susan Marchison. Sylvia and Susan both lost their husbands during the war.

Anna is a natural teacher. She has invented games to help our girls learn the English currency system. They give and receive coins, make change with pounds and shillings and do maths in the non-decimal monetary system. She tried to take them into the shops for practice but very few goods, beyond the barest necessities, are available for purchase.

The English find it difficult to accept this post-war austerity. The feeling that "we are all in it together fighting for victory" has been replaced with impatience. The indomitable spirit that kept them going against all odds is failing. Employment opportunities are few and far between and many still live in houses without windows, adequate furniture, or warmth.

To add to Britain's woes, the weather this winter is very harsh. The fallen snow does not melt and blocks roads and railways. Coal, already in short supply, cannot be delivered to fuel the power stations. Electricity has been cut to 19 hours a day and many industries have been forced to shut down completely, laying off 4,000,000 more workers. Television services are suspended and radio broadcasts are limited. Some magazines have been forced to cease publishing and our newspapers have become smaller. Unbelievably, food rations are now even lower than they were during the war.

The desperate situation here has turned the Minister of Fuel and Power, Emanual Shinwell, into a scapegoat. Death threats have made it necessary for him to move about the city under police protection. Our girls are the envy of the neighborhood with their warm American coats and we manage to stay well fed due to the generous gifts you added to their luggage.

Would that there was a GI Bill of Rights for British soldiers. I do not mention it to my neighbors. If they learned that returning U.S. soldiers are offered loans to buy a house, given tuition and living expenses if they chose to attend college or trade school, or given $20.00 per week for up to 52 weeks while they searched for work, they would no doubt become enraged.

In contrast, the unbombed factories in the U.S. are rapidly being converted to the production of automobiles and household goods. I am painfully aware of the current differences between the two countries.

After staying home for a few days to spend time with the girls, Thomas has returned to work. In a week or two he plans to arrive home in time to meet the girls after school on the days that I once again become an invisible watcher. Not until I reach London shall I be given the address of the flat that holds my wardrobe on that particular day. You assume correctly that I leave London and return to Highgate wearing my Mrs. Walker clothing.

When the weather improves, we shall plan a visit to Brackham Wood and the surrounding area. How wonderful it will be to meet with friends, introduce our girls, and show them my old haunts.

Maemi and Keiko have mailed letters to Catherine and they asked me to send their greetings to William and Bert and, of course, to you. Their new life here is exciting but they do miss you all.

I hope for an early springtime for you and am most eager to hear your news.

Love,
Moira

March 26, 1948

Dearest Moira,

The girls are so missed. We remark often on how "quiet the house is." But it is wonderful that they have a new friend to teach them the ropes, so to speak.

Catherine wants to try out for the newly organized Spokane Civic Theatre's production of *Tom Sawyer.* The play requires both adult and juvenile actors. However, my friend Dorothy Darby Smith, tells me that only North Central High School drama students will be considered for the younger parts as their drama teacher is the directress of this particular show. Dorothy would have first-hand information as she is the Chairman of the Civic Theatre Board. I suppose Catherine could try out for the Lewis and Clark, Spokane Children's Community Theatre's production of *The Wizard of Oz.* However, that may not be possible as Catherine, Bert and I are taking the train to Seattle for Easter. We'll be staying with Gillian and David. William will join us there and spend his vacation time only in Seattle. At the very least, we'll all be together, however brief the time is.

Bert is still working for the Public Library, but he has a new position. A couple of years ago, our library system initiated the use of a "bookmobile." The first Spokane traveling library was built by Brown Trailer for whom my cousin Gillian worked during the war years. Brown's first truck body was constructed from trailer parts and then outfitted as a bookmobile; what once was a cargo van has now become an aluminum library on wheels! Bert "rides" with the librarian and driver on Saturdays. He still works a couple of days after school in the downtown branch. The novelty of driving to different parts of the city while being with his beloved books makes him so happy.

You are so correct in your thoughts about how the GI Bill provisions would dishearten the people of Britain. Life for them, as well as for the four of you, sounds dreadful. At least here in the U.S., we are not faced with the reconstruction of bombed-out cities and countryside. Perhaps the provisions in *The Marshall Plan* will bring the United Kingdom some relief. Don't those loan monies start to flow next month?

The GI Bill is such a boon to our returned soldiers. I read a newspaper article a couple of weeks ago that stated that last year over 1500 homes were built in Spokane alone and 49 percent of college admissions are returning veterans who, instead of flooding the job market, have opted for an education. You might find it interesting to learn that many of the barracks from what was once Baxter Army Hospital are now sitting on Gonzaga, Whitworth, Eastern Washington State College and Spokane Public School campuses. They have been repurposed as classrooms, dormitories and student housing.

England's harsh winter, the suspension of communication services, the layoffs, food rationing and limited electricity are stark opposites to what is happening here. The U.S. seems to be on the move; construction is up, therefore employment is as well. Food is plentiful and we do not experience power limitations. The weather too, is a different story. In fact, today it is 45 degrees and later in the week the temperature is expected to rise even higher. Spring is not far off!

A National Health plan in Britain...do tell me more. Do you recall when National Health Insurance gained the support of President Truman in 1946? It quickly moved to the top of his priority list, but of all of his proposals, the only one that was ultimately successful was the proposal that provided federal funding for hospital construction. Some saw the passage as a compromise "forestalling incursions into areas of 'states rights' that might challenge the racial status quo." I wonder how long National Health Insurance and Civil Rights will be intertwined before one or the other or both are approved.

You don't actually believe that I would "propose" to Bill, do you? He is a very nice man, very much a gentleman, and excellent company, but at this moment I have no romantic aspirations, nor does he (I don't think). He travels often as a consultant and a visiting professor, but has regularly scheduled classes, which keep him primarily in Boston. I doubt that I will ever see him again, but my meeting was certainly more enjoyable because of his presence.

The George Butterick mystery seems to be solved. Julia called me at the office recently to tell me that the neighborhood was alive with the flashing lights of police cars; most of the activity was centered on the Butterick's home. Julia was worried that Catherine and Bert would arrive home from school and not be able to get through the police lines. I called their school and had a message delivered to the children. They came to the clinic after school. By the time we arrived home, there were still a couple of patrol cars in the driveway and the Butterick's house was fully lit. There was no sign of either Nancy, the children, or George.

In one of my earlier letters, I mentioned that I had seen George moving a truck, filled with what appeared to be frozen meat. George was a tire salesman but that was a cover story for something illegal. He was also involved with a group of felons dealing in the black market beef business in the eastern part of the state.

George would drive the truck to Montana where he would pick up a shipment of beef. He would then return to Spokane, park the truck (which was refrigerated) in his garage, and then a day or two later would deliver the truck's contents to designated restaurants and grocery stores throughout the city. Those businesses were buying the beef at extremely high prices. Apparently, many restaurants and grocers have been faced with having to pay black market prices in order to have beef to offer in their cases or on their menus. It wasn't just happening in Spokane; in fact, even small towns and other large cities across the state have been affected.

The rumor is that George was telling Nancy that he was delivering refrigerator trucks to their owners under the guise of having had the tires replaced and remounted, thereby allowing him to move about freely as both tire salesman and black marketeer.

George is now in jail awaiting trial; Nancy and the children have moved to her parents' home which is somewhere in Idaho. The house is still filled with furniture and other belongings. No one in our neighborhood seems to know what will happen next. I suppose I will never know whether the man on the train was George in disguise or just someone whose eyes resembled his. Your advice is appreciated as is that of Thomas; thanks to you both. Since George is in jail, I doubt that I shall have to worry about him any longer.

I am uncertain as to what should be made of a speech delivered here recently by State Senator Bienz. He declared that at least 150 of the approximately 700

University of Washington faculty members are Communists. Bienz is a member of the newly created Washington State Joint Legislative Fact-finding Committee on Un-American Activities. The committee is chaired by Albert Canwell, who is also from Spokane. Bienz said that there were over five million Communists or people who follow the Communist line living in the U.S. He ended the speech by saying, "Stalin intends to conquer the world and the United States." For the second time in our nation's history we have another "Red Scare." How far this one will go is anyone's guess, but we talk about it constantly at the clinic. There is always an article in the paper about it and I have to believe that it is the same in every city nation-wide. What about in London? What do you know about Communists there?

I look forward to hearing anything that Thomas learns from the "chaplain." After you first told me that Thomas was pursuing Charles' cause of death, it occurred to me that I will never be able to move on until I, too, know the cause. I merely accepted what we were told.

I must say that I am grateful that you now have the girls to keep you busy. I suppose you will only be out and about in disguise during the hours they are in school. What sort of plan is in place should you be delayed from getting home in time to greet them? Are you certain that your address is not "13 Rue de Madeleine?"

We send our love and prayers for your safety,

Margaret

April 13, 1948

My Dearest Margaret,

I am so happy to hear from you. I continue to miss our daily communication and often find myself thinking of something that I must tell Margaret this afternoon. Then I remember how far away you really are.

Your children are blooming. A bookmobile? What an interesting concept. I am so glad that Bert enjoys his work with the library and is embarking on a new venture. Who would ever think that libraries could move to the readers?

I am *gobsmacked* by the news of George Butterick. Never in my wildest imagination have I thought about black market beef in the U.S. Flashing lights and sirens on your street? In one way I wish I had been there to experience all the excitement. In another way I fear that I would have been plagued with memories of wartime London.

I was quite surprised by your news of the House Un-American Activities Committee chaired by Spokanite Albert Canwell although I probably should not have been. Both America and England were uneasy bedfellows of Russia during the past war. The Cold War has begun and I wish that it had not. We may not hear as much about it in this country because of our more immediate focus on day to day survival and restoring our infrastructure.

While one sector of the elite class in England was fascinated by Hitler and Fascism, another was mesmerized by Communism. The Communist party in England attracted members in the years before the war because of the country's economic depression, its rigid class system, the plight of the poor and Communists' strong stand against Fascism in Europe. The party's slogan "From each according to his ability, to each according to his needs" promises a heaven on earth: a classless society.

Therefore, upper class students studying in elite universities in England, particularly Cambridge, were fascinated by the concept and readily recruited into the Party. I try and try but I cannot fathom why brilliant young men who had been brought up in wealth and privilege were attracted to the idea. They had everything. Did they wish that they had been raised poor and hungry and servantless?

I love your sense of humor and your joke about our address being 13 Rue Madeleine. Happily, my life is neither as exciting nor as dangerous as those portrayed in that film. I cannot even imagine being involved in such dramatic events.

I have had two "days out" during which I went into central London and observed. My assignment was easy. I was given three places and the time to be at each. One was a Lyon's Tea Shop and another was a Lyon's Corner House. I was as invisible as a wren, the little bird that no one notices. What a contrast from New Year's Eve! I was free during the hour between assignments, which allowed me to gather my impressions and weave in and out of shops. I particularly enjoyed browsing the bookshops.

Thomas was with the girls when I arrived at our Highgate home. It was a joy to watch them interact with each other. He has assured me that he will be able to do that whenever I work long days. This makes me wonder if we are two people doing one job.

Now that the girls have settled in a bit and I have some time to myself, I revel in reading the letters you wrote to me between 1937 and 1945. I had impulsively thrown them into my old satchel as I packed for this move.

When our letters began I was maid-of-all-work living in Brackham Wood in this country and you were a thriving member of the medical profession with a husband and three children in Spokane, Washington. Your letters chronicle my metamorphosis from a timid woman with an impossible dream to a woman able to displace fear with courage and become part of her community. They also tell of your struggle to find your place in the medical community, to cope with your son's polio, and to manage without your husband after he left for war.

Reading your letters also reminded me of how eagerly we in England had looked forward to peace and a return to the glorious life we had led before the war. Even though that wonderful world may never have existed, its image propelled us through wartime. The reality in England is that food, building supplies, and clothing remain scarce and the job market struggles, despite an emergency loan from the U.S. of $3.75 billion. The additional Marshall Plan monies should soon begin to make a difference in this country's recovery.

Even those soldiers who had returned home to find their dwellings in one piece are facing difficulties. Some lost friends and relatives to dropped bombs, crumbling buildings, fire and the V-1 and V-2 rockets launched from Germany during the last year of the war. Others returned to their families to find them drastically changed. Their children did not recognize them and, possibly more disturbing, their wives were no longer the submissive girls they remembered. After years of making decisions on their own, women had learned to manage the household and the finances by themselves.

Some wartime marriages had been made in haste and soldiers returned only to realize that they barely knew the women they had married. Other husbands discovered that their wives' attitude for them had changed in their absence. Some married women had even developed feelings for other men.

Yesterday I finished reading one of the spy novels that I picked up while browsing Cambridge bookstores. In *The Great Impersonation* published in 1920, author E. Phillips Oppenheim writes of a German count and an English gentleman, both students at a school in England, who bore a close physical resemblance to one another and who seem to have switched identities in the years leading up to the Great War.

I realized with a shock that Oppenheim's novel reminded me of my own experience. As you remember my former employer, Harriet Malthorpe, worried me because she did not behave like a typical English woman. She was eventually revealed to be a German girl who had switched identities with an English classmate who had passed away while they were both enrolled in a Swiss boarding school.

As happened several times in our wartime correspondence, I must once again finish hastily and send this letter on. Something terrible has occurred that interrupts my reflections on the effects of war and, sadly, puts us in the middle of the story.

Sylvia, the mother of Maemi and Keiko's friend Anna, paid us an unexpected visit last evening while our girls were at her house with her daughter.

Sylvia is very concerned because her son, Ian, who has spent the last two months visiting his father's family in Yorkshire, will soon return to enter summer term. She fears that our girls will face discrimination when he returns. Ian's grandfather and uncles have been repeating stories of how badly the Japanese treated his father who was killed as a result of the "Fall of Singapore" in 1942. It was a terrible shock to this entire nation when Singapore fell. British soldiers outnumbered their Japanese opponents nearly three to one and yet they were defeated.

Before the war, the British believed that their fleet could relieve Singapore before any enemy had time to strike. However, the Japanese were able to effectively surround and cut them off, including their water supply. Being forced to surrender was a terrible blow to the British ego, particularly because the British had originally designed the water system that caused their defeat.

Anna and Ian's father survived being captured but many did not; the Japanese shot British soldiers as they climbed out of their trenches with their hands over their heads. He was then marched through Singapore where he was put in barracks and assigned to clean up the town. With his fellow soldiers he was forced to repair bomb-damaged roofs and buildings while being given scarce water and food.

After ten months of labor, they were regrouped and shipped to Taiwan in the hold of a ship. During the six-day trip, they were fed rotten food and given foul water. Their latrines were open buckets and dysentery was rife. Upon landing, their boots were taken and they were force marched for a day wearing only flimsy rubber shoes.

Sick and weak, they were put to work in copper mines in freezing temperatures. After being given a small can of rice and a cup of water, they slept but were soon awakened and marched to the work site. Anna and Ian's father was beaten to death when he became too weak to pick up his drill. Ian's grandfather and uncles have learned of his terrible death during the past few weeks and talk about it constantly. In his letters, Ian displays his rage as only a boy of that age can do. He writes hateful things about all the Japanese, even threatening to kill the first one he sees.

Sylvia now regrets having sent him to be with his father's family. She had not wanted him to go. However, he begged and she relented when she realized that he could be a help to them as they struggled with the loss of their son and brother.

I remember my concern when you first told me that Maemi and Keiko had come to live in your house. I feared that there would be retribution at that time. Happily there was none.

We have only weeks before Ian returns and are in a complete quandary as to what to do. Our immediate reaction is to flee back to Spokane, the community that seems safe and secure. Until a person has children of their own, they never realize to what lengths they would go to protect them from injustice and indignity.

You can see my dilemma. I am ready to pack our bags, desert Eileen's house, leave my native country and return home. Thomas, too, is very upset. Perhaps we were unrealistic in thinking that we can spare them. So now you can see that we have many decisions to make and need to embark on a search for the best way to handle this. We are very grateful to Sylvia for coming to us. Of course, she is also very disturbed by the entire situation and how it has affected her son.

Please send our love to all.

Moira
Thomas asked me to add his name and his regards to this letter.

April 30, 1948

My Dearest Moira,

You must be having a good laugh over some of my past letters! If it weren't so costly, I would send you yours; then you'd really have fun! Our early writing years were so innocent and then came the war! I don't like to think of where you might be had you not sent that very first letter!

Ian Bradbury's life is such a sad story, a child who has taken on the hatred of his parent and relatives. It distresses me to think of how his return could affect your family. I suppose there are similar stories here in the U.S., but I have heard nothing like the venom you have described. Of course, you will not expose the girls to a situation where he may be able to lash out at them. It's doubly troubling as the girls have become such friends of Anna. Ian could poison that relationship as well. You and Thomas will do the right thing. If it means leaving Eileen's house and returning to Spokane, then so be it. Are you and Eileen in contact with one another? Perhaps you could sublet the house? I'm certain that Thomas knows of, or can find help in finding a responsible party to lease the house in your stead.

You, indeed, are no longer the timid woman of years ago; most certainly you have grown into the antithesis of that woman! I reluctantly accept how you can be out prowling the streets while the girls are otherwise occupied with school. Thank goodness Thomas can be so flexible in his work that he is able to be home to greet the girls if you have yet to return. What do you expect to see in the places you are sent? Who is watching out for you? Was there any feeling of déjà vu being in Lyon's Tea Shop, the scene of the accident that nearly killed you years ago? By the way, how eerily the plot of *The Great Impersonation* mimics real life. I dimly recall the wartime movie of the same name, but I don't think I saw it. I must ask Bert to look for the book at the library.

Our trip to Seattle at Easter was great fun, although Catherine stayed in Spokane. Sarah and Lloyd Jacobs offered to spend the long weekend at our house as Julia had made other plans. I felt assured that Catherine would be well-cared for and knew that Sarah would see to her transportation to play practice. (Yes, she got a part after all.) It is a wonderful experience for her.

Bert, William and I stayed with Gillian and David. It was wonderful to be with them and to begin plans for our summer at Newman Lake. We went to Easter Sunday Mass at St. Mark's, the Cathedral in which they had been married. We then went to the Olympic Hotel in downtown Seattle, for an early dinner.

The hotel is absolutely gorgeous. It sits in the middle of the downtown area on a piece of property known as the Metropolitan Tract. The property was once was the home of the University of Washington. The hotel itself was built with public subscription, however the property and the hotel are owned by the University.

The interior is lovely. We ate in the Georgian Room, which is furnished with dark walnut furniture everywhere in the public areas and with damask and velour draperies on the windows. Huge chandeliers light the space. David put Bert and me back on the train later in the evening and we were home early Monday morning.

William stayed in Seattle for an extra couple of days. David took him to the Boeing Plant to show him his office. William learned that the Aeronautical Machinists may strike any day. I didn't think that college students would be interested in that information, but I suppose a journalism major might well be. Contract negotiations have been going on for over a year; the Boeing Company and the Machinists as well, refuse to budge and things are coming to a head. William told me that the dinner conversation that night was very animated when Gillian interjected that Boeing "wanted blanket disqualification of women from open jobs if, in the Boeing Company's opinion, the job required a man." Oh, my goodness! I can just imagine the fire in her eyes! My future journalist says that he has a great topic for a required term paper.

Spring has arrived in Spokane. The lilacs are beginning to bud as well as the syringas and forsythias. I'm particularly happy to see the snow disappear as I have been invited by Joe Parsons and his wife, Delores, to visit them in Pasco. I met Joe when I was there in January for a State Medical Society visitation. Joe is a Boarded Pediatrician and the treasurer of the State Society.

It's warmer at this time of year in Pasco than in Spokane. I'm hoping to be able to play some friendly tennis with Delores. I haven't played for years, but she understands that and promises not to push me too hard!

Your home looks lovely; I drove by recently to check on the property. The renters planted tulip and daffodil bulbs in the front beds last fall that are now just beginning to peek out. Someone was washing the windows; perhaps the renter?

Moira, I do hope all is resolved peacefully for Maemi's and Keiko's sakes. Who would have ever imagined that they could become targets of such hatred? I suppose their lives were very sheltered from that here in Spokane, though I am not so naive as to think that there is no hatred here. The war continues long after it has ended, doesn't it?

You are in my thoughts and prayers!

Love,
Margaret

May 15, 1948

My Dearest, Dearest Margaret,

I am so happy to hear from you. Your last letter began with a powerful question. I dread to think where I would be if I had not sent you that first letter. Your support was a lifeline. Your suggestions and nudges gave me courage. I became brave enough to meet my neighbors, operate a vehicle, plant a victory garden, travel to London, investigate the strange behavior of my employers, meet my husband, travel to the U.S. and adopt our two precious daughters.

I could add much more to this paean of praise if I were not fairly bursting with news. The first, and most important, is that as a result of Thomas' tireless pursuit of information about his brother, we were put in contact with Rev. Richard Smith, who served as a chaplain with the Timberwolf Division.

Thomas' and my long, cordial and emotional meeting with the former chaplain began with a lengthy narration of the part that the 104th Infantry Division played in the war. The Timberwolves achieved splendid success, never failing to attain an objective on schedule. They blocked the enemy and mopped up after battles. They advanced as many as

140 miles in a single week until, after six months and 18 days of combat, they met up with the Russian 118th Division on April 27, 1945.

The Timberwolves had outstanding teamwork, moved quickly, and made bold night attacks; they used an L-4 Piper Cub for observation of the enemy. Being in the air in such a small aircraft was a dangerous business. It has occurred to me that William and Bert particularly would like to hear these combat stories.

Richard's powers of description were almost too vivid. I must confess that, as I sat there listening to his tales of combat, they became so visceral that I wanted to run screaming from the room several times. They horrify me even now as I write.

Only after he finished describing the technical activities of the division did he reveal to us that he knew Charles personally. He held your husband in great esteem. The two men met after Chaplain Smith had performed a quick Mass on Christmas Eve with distant gunfire illuminating the far horizon. As usual, the men scattered quickly after the last word. However, Charles remained behind to help Richard pack his kit, which contained book, chalice, host dish, candlesticks, cross and a small portable wooden altar about 14 inches high and eight inches wide that was hinged to lie flat.

Charles' presence comforted Richard. The main activities of a chaplain are giving last rites and holding services whenever possible. In that position they have virtually no peers unless they find another officer of like mind. He had found such a friend in Charles.

The Timberwolves were always on the move and he appreciated Charles' powers of observation as well as his ability to put situations in perspective. He was not surprised when he learned that Charles was a journalist by profession. Charles told Richard much about his family, describing his brilliant, effective, efficient and loving wife and talked of his children as though they were the best in the world. A tear formed in the corner of Richard's eye as he described conducting Last Rites for Charles, who was hit by a bullet during the last hours of the war in Europe, May 8. He died two days later. Technically he lived through the war.

Thomas thanked Richard for his sincere and earnest testimonial to his brother, walked him to the door, shut it, returned to the parlor and broke down completely. At first I felt as if my tower of strength had crumbled. Then slowly the memories of how you cared for me began to flood back. After his long pursuit of the truth about Charles, I recognized that he was in shock as I had been. Thanks to your example in caring for me when I arrived at your doorstep three years ago, the girls and I both knew how to care for him. It took two or three days before I once again began to see a glimmer of the man I knew.

He emerged a changed man. He announced that he wanted all of us to return to the U.S. in the near future. He would like to return to full-time journalism and is targeting possible placements in Oak Ridge, Tennessee, Los Alamos, New Mexico, and Richland, Washington. Of course, you know which placement I hope for. Richland would be so close to you.

My work continues. I do not feel that I am in danger as I go about my ramblings. It is easy to feel invisible in such large crowds. I have learned to move with the crowd. I walk looking straight ahead or with my eyes cast slightly downward. I always wear a hat and dress in neutral colors and occasionally wear glasses. If something draws the attention of the crowd, I move my gaze to mimic that of the others.

Other watchers go to great trouble to avoid being followed. They double back, change tube lines, go from bus to tube to train to bus. It is my observation that they often end up several hours later very close to the place where their journey began.

The girls seem to be coping well with their classes at Camden School for Girls. They enjoy being there even though the school days are longer, and the teachers, subject matter, games and sports are all new to them. They seem to tolerate wearing school uniforms without much complaint. They were, however, surprised when they learned that every school day was to begin with chapel.

The planets seem to lining up in our favor as we also have just heard from Eileen. Sadly, her sister passed away sooner than expected. Her surgery had been successful but her recovery lagged. They have not determined the exact cause of her death. Eileen will return to her Highgate home when she feels that all is settled there.

Should time allow, we shall all visit Brackham Wood before we leave the country. Patricia Dimblebey has offered us accommodation in the rectory. We would like very much to go but we shall see.

Although a short letter, I will post it immediately as I want you to hear of Charles.

Much love,
Moira

May 28, 1948

Dearest Moira,

Though Charles never spoke of Chaplain Smith in any of his letters, I am pleased to have your news of Thomas having met with him. It is comforting to know that Charles was not alone when he was struck down and that he received Last Rites. It is also a relief to know that Thomas is now free of the burden, which has haunted him for three years, the older son who could not stop fate from taking his kid brother. I don't quite know how to describe what I feel. I suppose it is relief knowing what really happened, but at the same time there is a gnawing, haunting anger, that Charles died in the last hours of the war. A sniper perhaps?

I cannot believe that Thomas is ready to resume his journalism career full-time and to return to the U.S.! It's absolutely amazing. And all because he solved the mystery of Charles' death? What about you? What about the work that you have just begun, at his suggestion, I might add? How can you just pull out of that after a mere few weeks of observations? I wonder whether you actually saw something or someone whose value you do not understand, but Thomas does, and now your work is ended!

The thought of you living somewhere other than Spokane leaves me with a feeling of great emptiness. I do hope his new position is in Richland. At least then, you would be a mere two hundred miles or so away, instead of the huge distance between here and either New Mexico or Tennessee. Bells went off when I read the names of the three choices in which to resume his journalism career! What is located in any of those cities that would motivate him to intentionally choose any of those places? What newspaper exists in any of those three cities that could possibly be comparable to the *Review?*

Sarah and her husband Lloyd Jacobs are in the process of trying to make the move to Israel. I suspect the plan has been in the works for months, but now that the British mandate for Palestine is coming to an end and Jewish leaders have proclaimed the establishment of the State of Israel, their emigration is picking up speed. I believe that the Hadassah Massacre last month persuaded them they had to do something. Seventy-eight Jewish doctors, nurses, students, patients, faculty members and Haganah fighters, and one British soldier were killed in the attack. Dozens of unidentified bodies, burned beyond recognition, were buried in a mass grave in the Sanhedria Cemetery. Since Sarah and Jacob have no children I suppose they are free to move to a place of such unrest without fear for little ones. Again I wonder, "Why would they?"

Catherine, Bert and I opened the cottage at Newman Lake last weekend. Gillian and David came from Seattle to open their cottage as well. At days'end we gathered for dinner, Friday night at their cottage, then on Saturday at ours. The main topic of conversation during the weekend was the restrictive covenant that is in force on the house which the Stewarts own in Broadmoor, a housing area in Seattle.

When David and his first wife bought the house, they were unaware of the covenant's restrictions, only that a "covenant" existed. Now that Gillian and he have decided to sell the house, they have discovered what the actual terms are. The Supreme Court holds that restrictive covenants are illegal and that the Government could not help to enforce them. However, this left open a loophole—the possibility of voluntary agreements between realtors and homeowners which allowed housing discrimination to continue. The original owners of the house signed such an agreement and it appears that it is still in force.

We spent the weekend, preparing the cottage for the summer. I have renters for the months of June and July. I intend to keep the entire month of August for ourselves. Perhaps you will be home by then. If you are not in the midst of a move, we can just loll the month away together.

I had a great time in Pasco last month with Joe and Dolores Parsons. My tennis game is not the best, but I enjoyed the romp on the court nonetheless. They took me by car as close as we could get to the Hanford Project gates. It's so eerie and isolated. There is something frightening about just being in its shadow! The Parsons didn't seem to be bothered by the area.

We then drove a few more miles to the site of a canal from which water will be pumped for the first time later this month onto a Pasco farm. This water is the result of the dreams of many to irrigate the region. Hopefully, the ability to irrigate this arid dust bowl will transform it into lush agricultural land. The canal is in sharp contrast to the home of the Atomic Bomb!

Not only was my short trip a morale booster, but I suspect it was one for the Parsons, as well. Their youngest son has been undergoing thyroid treatments. It's very unusual for a child to have thymus issues. I wondered whether it could be the result of exposure to the releases from the Hanford Project. We know so little about the damages to air quality from that site, or from any of others that belch fog into the atmosphere. The people who live in that area don't seem to question it at all. I suppose that is because the area is booming and the economy is as well. But really, who knows how far the winds carry those releases? I know I must sound like a nay-sayer, considering all the jobs that the Project has brought to the area. But seriously, do any of us really know what the gunk we put into the atmosphere is doing to the environment, let alone what it does to humans?

If there is anything that I can do to help make your return home easier, you need only ask. If you intend to sell your house here, I can contact a realtor to get the ball rolling.

I, too, have been considering a move. Nothing to announce yet, just looking!

Larry Blanchard seems to be healing. He has been playing golf again and is beginning to enjoy the cottage at which he and Karen had so much joy. He is hosting a party in a couple of weeks to celebrate the five-year anniversary of the Montrose Clinic. He has asked me to be his hostess and of course I will do so. (I think that he has been seeing a nurse who works at Sacred Heart Hospital, but that seems to be something he keeps to himself. He might have asked her, but curiously he didn't. Maybe he's not ready.)

And now to sleep; morning comes too soon. Before I know it, I am back at the office.

I look forward to hearing of your plans. Again, if there is anything I can do to help, please let me do so. And please lobby hard for Richland!!!!

With love,

Margaret

Brackham Wood
Monday, June 14, 1948

My Dearest Margaret,
   Thank you for your most welcome letter. Last week Thomas told us that we will almost definitely be moving to Tennessee, New Mexico, or Richland.

He will say no more. The girls and I have our hearts set on being close to you, despite your description of that part of the country as an arid dust bowl and the Hanford site as eerie and isolated. Near you is where our hearts lie and I truly hope we get there sooner rather than later.

I am glad to hear that the Parsons are happy in Pasco. I knew that you would enjoy your visit with them. I picture you a vision of grace on the tennis court and suspect that you played better than you are willing to admit. The story of their young son's health issues is, of course, disconcerting. However, I do not find it surprising that the people living near the Hanford Nuclear Reactor fail to question its possible dangers. I hear that Hanford employees are well paid and the schools in Richland very good. Those who choose to go there must feel that the rewards outweigh the possible dangers. I doubt if the powers that be even mention such a possibility.

Thomas remembers seeing an August, 1945 copy of Richland's newspaper, *The Villager*, with headlines screaming: "IT'S ATOMIC BOMBS." Only then did Hanford employees learn the purpose of their work. They were jubilant. Until that day they knew only that they were working on something secret and important to the defense of the country. Of course there are dangers involved with every new scientific discovery and you are wise to be concerned about emissions from Hanford. We may not learn the consequences for many years.

I believe that Sarah and her husband will make a difference in the creation and stability of the State of Israel. Imagine what will be involved in the creation of a new country. Hearing of the massacre is most distressing. Is it possible that we will live to see the end of wars? I sincerely hope so but have my doubts.

I remember that what we now call "The Great War" or "World War I" was once referred to as the "War to End All Wars." How well we now know that it was not.

Thank you for your offer to help in our resettlement. I know that you will once again be a lifesaver for us. Just now our minds are full of hypotheses, and questions and more questions but we feel excited and have energy. I am very relieved that we will return to the United States as is Thomas. He seems years younger than he did three months ago. I do not know if that is caused by the promise of a change in our location or by uncovering the truth about his brother's death. Even a sad discovery is better than a mystery.

Putting his mind to rest about Charles seems to have freed Thomas from a burden he has carried for the past two years. He talks with Chaplain Smith often and as a family we have attended Sunday services when and where Rev. Smith serves as a visiting priest. These visits have taken me to parts of London I have neither seen nor heard tell of. We travel to theses services by tube. Maemi and Keiko love these journeys. Burrowing around underground is new to them and they love scrambling up the stairs and, as they word it, "popping up into a new world."

I am so glad that you are able to enjoy the lake early this year and that Gillian and David could do so as well. It is a place of beauty and peace. At times during these past few difficult weeks I have calmed myself by closing my eyes and imagining the restful scene on the other side of the cabin window. I had not realized that Gillian and David are about to sell their house and I must admit that the thought of restrictive covenants came as a shock, particularly because of what we continue to learn about recent events in Germany.

I am surprised that you are looking for another home but feel confident that you will be able to find just the right house even in the booming U.S. market.

The Montrose Clinic party may be an event of the past by the time you read this. I am anxious to read your description of the event. The hint of a nurse in the picture is a bit puzzling. If she does exist perhaps she will be invited as a guest.

Even though our lives are in an upheaval just now I am truly glad that we are here with the girls. They will have a new worldview when they return to the United Sates. I continue to be amazed at and grateful for their ability to adjust to new surroundings. Your intervention at a critical time in their lives has made all the difference. The shock and horror of losing their parents was greatly muffled by the love with which your family quickly and lovingly enveloped them.

I experienced the same thing as I emerged from my state of shock in your home. Even with no idea of where I was, I felt completely safe, loved and cared for—a security that I had not felt since before my parents' deaths 25 years earlier. I can think of no proper way to thank you.

Thomas has recently been working as a researcher. He has spent time in the Public Records Office and Somerset House as well as at the BBC. Just now he has a great deal of autonomy. I have been on another observation, this time back at Cambridge. I have discovered that the shopkeepers in the town know, and are most willing to talk about the students, particularly those who come from famous families.

When these upper class boys were young they were cosseted by their nannies. Then suddenly, at the age of eight, they were sent away from home to elite boys' schools such as Eton and Harrow where the older boys taught them how to behave using unkind and even abusive methods. They formed strong bonds with their classmates as a type of survival. By the time they got to Cambridge University they had made lifelong connections with one another, which followed them throughout their professional and personal lives.

As you see, this letter is written from Brackham Wood. Tomorrow morning we will return home after a four-day visit, which began on Friday and will last until we step on the train. Having been frightened by Ian's attitude, we feared that we may have needed to cut this visit short. Happily, however, just the opposite was true.

The village children treated Maemi and Keiko like film stars. They are seen as exotic creatures from another land. A large crowd of children of all ages followed them wherever they wandered. Shortly after we arrived, they were invited to visit the village school. Yesterday they talked about life in the U.S. to every class and, at the end of the day, they gave a dramatic reading to the assembled student body.

The attention they received reminds me of two incidents in my own life. The first was the day I came to Brackham Wood with new husband Thomas and was given a surprise wedding reception. The second was in Spokane shortly after I began to venture out of your house. People gathered round to hear me speak. I am happy for the girls that they have had this small taste of celebrity. It makes me feel better about this mad and unsettled time in our family life: our setting off without them, their journey of thousands of miles to join us and now our impending return to the States.

Physically the village is nearly unchanged since before the war. Unlike London, no rubble lies along the roads. No ruins stand in place of buildings. The trenches dug into the village green in 1938 remain; the once bare canal is now grown over with greenery. The village children seem to use it as a place to play; hiding and jumping up to surprise their friends.

There is little evidence that any American Army Air Corps bases ever existed in the surrounding countryside. All that remains are the occasional cement pad or a bit of fencing that has not yet been put to another purpose by nearby farmers. I, however, remember delivering countless loads of building materials to these sites while driving a lorry held together with bailing wire and twine. That broken down and now plundered vehicle sits exactly where I last parked it over five years ago. Climbing into and out of the seat in that lorry forced me to become one of the first women in the village to wear trousers.

The village shops are much the same with the exception of the empty storefront where the Women's Volunteer Service Thrift Shop once stood. The homes and gardens are unchanged. The Anderson Shelters stand where they were erected. Some are abandoned while others are maintained and used for storage.

While the village looks much the same, the lives of nearly all the villagers have been irreversibly altered. The one exception seems to be my former employer, George Malthorpe, who maintains his daily routine exactly as he did ten years ago. Each morning he walks to his haberdashery, opens the door at 9:00, locks it at 13:00 for lunch, unlocks it again at 14:00 and welcomes customers until 18:00. At 18:30 he begins his walk home. Patricia Dimblebey told me that people who live along his route set their clocks by his daily movements.

Yesterday we visited him at Michelsgrove, his family home. He seemed extraordinarily happy to see us. I should not have been surprised that nothing had changed in that house since I left. George maintains his cottage garden exactly as I planted it. The flower-patterned overstuffed chair and settee look just as they did the day they were delivered from the upholsterers in 1935. I was able to show the girls the modifications that were made to the plumbing after I began working there. They laughed heartily when I showed them the inside door to the toilet that had been installed only after I moved in.

George's former brother-in-law, Malcolm, continues to celebrate Christmas with him each year. Much to George's amusement, Malcolm seems to be enjoying the company of several of the many women widowed by the war. Each year he brings a different one with him to celebrate the holiday in Brackham Wood.

Henry and Lucy Grimes, who came here as evacuees from London, were never claimed by their parents. They continue to live with and work for James and Hattie Johnson, the brother and sister who adopted them.

Jeb Hastings, the foreman on the crew who dug the trenches in the village green, is unable to work because of his war injuries and I was told that he has become quite taciturn. His wife Marie cares for him and adds to their meager resources by working as a waitress at Cole's Tea Shop. She lost track of both of her daughters after they eloped with American servicemen. She refuses to speak of either of them.

Reverend Vincent Dimblebey and Patricia have been gracious hosts to our family. The church was full yesterday and the after-service fellowship was a real celebration. I was happy to learn that members of the parish continue to donate ration coupons and treats for the after-service gathering. The prayer box, introduced during wartime, is still in use. I remember how the parishioners hesitated to insert their written prayer requests into the slot in that box when it first stood in front of the altar rail. Now there is no hesitation. I joined the line that formed before the service began. I requested prayers for all of us in the Walker family.

We shall see what the next week brings. Perhaps Eileen will return. Perhaps Thomas will hear of some new opportunities. Perhaps all our concerns will be sorted out neatly. Perhaps it will not be neat but they will eventually be sorted out.

I imagine that you have celebrated yet another Lilac Festival. I miss you and look forward to your next letter.

Love,
Moira

June 30, 1948

Dearest Moira,

Although our letters are frequent, it is still difficult waiting until I receive word from you!

How wonderful that you were able to return to Brackham Wood! I am reasonably certain that the contrast between Spokane and the village was startling. Nevertheless to be able to see dear friends must have been emotionally gratifying. I suspect you yourself thought you would never again see England, let alone Brackham Wood.

Despite the flux in your lives you haven't given up "observing," though I can't fathom why young Cambridge students are your subjects. One thing I do know is that it has to be important to our government or you wouldn't be tramping in and out of shops. Have you learned any good gossip about famous families or their scions? I can visualize you chatting with shopkeepers and picking up some juicy tidbit!

Moira, there are many job opportunities in this state, the Pasco/Hanford area being one of them. However, I think that it is not a place for a journalist of Thomas' caliber. Since he wants to make a career change, I think he would be much better off seeking a job in a large city. What about a different journalistic direction? What about television?

Why is he being so secretive about where you are to move? Don't you have a say in where it is to be? It's none of my business, I suppose, but have you even discussed the three spots other than to have him say that he is going to resume his journalism career in one of them? This is so unlike the Thomas I once knew. He is definitely a man of many faces. The man I knew would never have refused to say nothing more than "we're definitely going to either Tennessee, New Mexico, or Washington."

During my travels to the southeastern part of the state for the Medical Society, I saw few pretty treed streets in the towns and cities. The three cities of Kennewick, Pasco and Richland are arid and flat. Sagebrush and mesquite grow in abundance. Only in the higher elevations would one find pines; even there the land is dry and dusty. Of course, now that water is a reality throughout the region as a result of the Columbia Basin Irrigation System, you could conceivably create your own Eden just as you did in Brackham Wood. I could never, ever consider living anywhere in the Tri-City area. I can't imagine you living there either! New Mexico has the same type of conditions as the Richland area and Tennessee would be hot and humid!

To bide his time, Thomas is now doing research in Public Records? For what purpose? Is he doing the same type of "research" in Somerset House? I thought that building housed something to do with Revenue and Probate. I am so frustrated not having a clear decision about where you are to go and what it is that Thomas will be doing there. I don't know how you can stand all the unknowns!

Bert's graduation was a wonderful day for all of us. He was chosen by his classmates to give the Commencement speech. We were so proud of him! Two of his female classmates have been accepted at Gonzaga University already. The newspaper reports that a total of 70 females are registered for the coming year. One male student said that he was worried that the women would be "the smartest in the class." This September will mark the end of Gonzaga's 61 years as a male-only school. The girls will be required to live with relatives as there is no dormitory for them. I wonder when they will start building one.

Bert can hardly contain himself as he thinks of starting pre-med studies at Northwestern in September. I am excited as well to have him join his brother at his grandfather's and my Alma Mater. He will maintain his bookmobile job until mid August. Then he will spend several days at the lake and return home just in time to finish his packing. I plan to go with him to Chicago to check on Mummy and Father's house and to see that he gets settled. I don't think he wants me anywhere near his fraternity, so I will make myself as scarce as possible.

I am considering the possibility of selling Mummy and Father's house in the next couple of years. Though I have an excellent property manager, I believe that it is time to sell the "grand lady." So much of the area is already being incorporated into Northwestern's campus. This may be a good time to sell.

Now to the Montrose Party…Larry's cottage is at Lake Coeur d'Alene. Reaching it is difficult as the road is unpaved and one must walk down several steps to get to the shore. But once arriving at level ground, it is worth the effort as his view is magnificent. He has at least 100 feet of beach frontage shared with only one other cottage. His bungalow cottage sits at the shoreline; the lapping of the water can be heard from inside. There is a large grassed area adjacent to the beach; that is where we partied from about noon to eight.

We roasted hotdogs over an open fire pit, then toasted marshmallows which we put on a graham cracker, topped with a piece of Hershey's chocolate, then made a sandwich out of the concoction by topping it with another graham cracker. It's an old Girl Scout recipe called, "Some More." I felt as if I were back at Camp!

Larry's nurse friend was nowhere to be seen. Rumor has it that she had two former husbands who died under mysterious circumstances. Both spouses left her well-provided-for, but the inquest regarding the second husband's death is due to begin in late August and she may be indicted. I don't know where Larry met her or how involved he is/was with her. I can't imagine what he is/was thinking! Since she wasn't there, perhaps he has come to his senses! I must pursue this further. The whole matter disgusts me! I thought he was healing!!!

The clinic group has been talking growth and what the next five years will mean to Montrose. We are all painfully aware that now that the "South Center" and "Southwest" wings of Sacred Heart Hospital are nearly completed, not much room remains for parking for our patients or even for those of the hospital for that matter.

The hospital is bordered on the north by wonderful old homes like Louis Davenport's, now the Porter's house, which has an enormous amount of landscaped property. It would be criminal to turn that into a parking lot! One of the other houses on that same street is owned by Mary and Peter Gianetsas. It is located on the corner of McClellan and 8th. There is a beautiful sunroom on the west side of the home that she and her husband built last year where Mary sits and looks out over the parking lot. They had no use for the lawn, but needed some extra income so the story goes. They now charge twenty-five cents to park in their lot. It has been noted that Mary will rap on the window if someone tries to park and not pay.

The land behind Larry's family home on Ninth Avenue, which has become our clinic, is undeveloped but not for sale. This means we would have to leave the current site and move further away from Sacred Heart to expand for both a clinic and the necessary parking. Being in the shadow of the hospital has been so convenient. I hope that we can find a piece of property in the vicinity.

My vacation begins in just a few more weeks. I am so looking forward to the chance to rest and do next-to-nothing! The latter won't happen as there is always something to be done, but somehow it is different when one is at "The Lake." I'm ready to be lazy! Would that you could join us!

Love,

Margaret

P.S. The Lilac Festival was a success with lovely spring temperatures! We had been worried about the weather as many parts of the Northwest have been experiencing a rapid snow melt which resulted in flooding.

July 17, 1948

My Dearest Margaret,

How wonderful to find a letter from you among the four that arrived in this morning's post. Along with your most welcome message, I received one from our landlady Eileen, one from Emily Mayview, and one in a thick paper envelope bearing the return address of Edith Elizabeth Elliott written in a beautiful hand. I have rarely seen and certainly never personally received a letter in such an envelope.

The thought of Bert graduating from high school shocks me to the core. We were very sorry to miss the event and hope that he has received the gift we sent him. What a testament that his classmates chose him to address them at Commencement. I remember the concern I felt for him as he struggled to survive and overcome polio and my amazement at how well he adjusted, always trying to keep up with the others and finding a way to serve others as he recovered. I predict a bright future for him as I do for all of our children.

Your news of young women becoming part of the student body at Gonzaga University amazes me. I admire them for their courage. I doubt their road will be easy. Cambridge University only began to allow women to earn degrees last year. Heavens, in 1905 when we were born, women were not allowed to vote in either England or America. English women were given the vote in 1918 but not until they were 30 years old. I cast my first vote in England in 1928 at age 23 when that age was lowered to 21. In the U.S. you cast your first vote in 1927 when you were 22. The world is changing.

Thank you for your impressions of Kennewick, Pasco, and Richland. Apparently not every part of Washington fits its "Evergreen State" nickname. Living close to you is a powerful pull but we will certainly take your description to heart.

The Montrose Clinic Lake party sounds like so much fun. I know that you were a perfect hostess and the activities and food you planned made for a great time. What a joy to return to the carefree days of childhood when one is a responsible adult.

I do wonder what could be in Larry's mind. Perhaps many years with a faithful and reliable wife left him defenseless against a woman who, from your description, possesses neither of those qualities. A nurse whose two former husbands died under mysterious circumstances? This sounds like a plot that comes directly from an Agatha Christie novel, and sheds an eerie light on her absence from the party.

No doubt your clinic will soon find a good home. I predict that you will have some influence in choosing the new location and, that said, I know it will be a good choice.

I have spent one more day as a "Watcher." I am beginning to think that my work is intended to teach me to recognize the regular rhythm of a particular area so that I shall be able to detect unusual activity. Perhaps they ask me to do this because they want a woman's perspective. I enjoy writing my reports and assume that they are acceptable because I am being given successive assignments.

To answer your question about Cambridge, I have overheard stories about a family whose handsome son graduated with a degree in Economics from Trinity College during the last decade. His father, St. John Philby, had also studied at Trinity College and had been in the Arab world with T. E. Lawrence, whose nickname was "Lawrence of Arabia." On another day I overheard two undergraduates mention that one of the queen's cousins also studied at Trinity College. Names are not used but I imagine that, with a little research, I could discover them. Perhaps when the pace of our life slows down I shall do that.

Maemi, Keiko and Thomas all seem to have benefitted from our trip to Brackham Wood. Thomas continues his pursuit of job opportunities "back in the states" as he words it. The girls are doing well here even though they long to see Catherine. I know that they correspond frequently with her though I seriously doubt that their letters describe London or learning to negotiate pounds sterling.

Now I must tell you about the letter I found within the expensive envelope. The formality of the letter startled me as did the beautiful hand in which it was written and signed by Edith Elizabeth Elliott. In the course of the letter she described her circumstance in great detail, explaining that she was in great turmoil because she was faced with a very important decision. She had first gone to Susan Marchison, her old school friend and the aunt of Maemi and Keiko's friend, Anna, to discuss her dilemma. Susan suggested that I could, perhaps, offer her a helpful perspective regarding her future.

I paused after reading her introduction. I felt like a character in a play. Here was I, a former maid, being asked for advice by a woman who wrote on such paper with such handwriting. As I continued to read I became even less confident that I could be of help to her. She related that when the war broke out she had been a 19-year-old gentleman's daughter living at home in comfort and boredom. She quickly signed up to train as a nurse.

At first she had been shocked to discover what was required of her. She had expected to tend officers by bathing their sweating brows and serving tea. In reality, however, she was asked to empty and clean bedpans and bathe and handle the raw wounds of soldiers of all ranks. With time, however, she became inured to the blood, bandages and bedpans. She relished her work and did not miss the protected life of her childhood. At war's end she trained to become a dispenser.

Thus began her dilemma. While working in a hospital pharmacy she met and became fond of an American doctor and he of her. Martin Evans has remained in England in hopes of convincing her to move to his home country. He has told her that he plans to return to the U.S. and take a position at a hospital in Richland, Washington. He is running out of patience and she is running out of time.

When Susan told her that she knew an English-born woman currently living in England and planning to return to the U.S., Edith Elizabeth became anxious to speak with me. Even more amazed was she to hear that I had lived in the State of Washington. She had assumed that Martin was from the nation's capital until he showed her a map.

She wrote in hopes that I would be willing to meet with her in a very nice tearoom in London.

I am about to reply in the affirmative. Even though not of her class, I can put on my "toney" accent and possibly be of some help in describing the world she would be entering. I am resolved not to advise her. However, to you I will confess that, if I were I to advise her, I would urge her to take the chance. The shortage of healthy Englishmen and my good luck with Thomas would recommend that she make the move. Also, at the age of 28, she is becoming quite ripe on the vine. As you know, I was even riper but I had a cousin on my side. Chances do not come that frequently.

However, I can advise her on life in America. She would be surprised to learn that, in the U.S., such a formal letter as she sent me would not be needed. She could probably stop anyone on the street and ask what they thought of her predicament and receive many candid and varying answers.

The third letter was from our landlady Eileen who hopes to return to this house in a few weeks. Currently she is heavily involved in settling the estate of her sister and has run upon some thorny problems revolving around the distribution of assets to various relatives. She states that the assets are few but, in this difficult time in England, they are badly needed by several family members. She confesses that having been a schoolmistress is a big help. When necessary she can assume an authoritative air that puts a stop to all discussion and disagreement.

The last of the four letters was from Emily Mayview, who, you may remember, was a child in the first family that employed me as a maid-of-all work. I heard that she had married an American G.I. and settled in our state. Indeed, her husband's family had been ejected precipitously from their farm in White Bluffs, Washington, in 1942 and resettled near Ritzville. She wrote me a brief letter, giving only her new address.

If I believed in omens, I would see today's morning mail as a call back to Washington. But I fear that it is too late to see you at the lake this year but I am confident we will do so next year.

Write soon, dear cousin, and let me know what is going on there.

Much love,
Moira and Thomas, Maemi and Keiko

August 3, 1948

Dearest Moira,

I so enjoyed your last letter. It sounds as if your world is moving fast enough to break the sound barrier. Between "outings" in Cambridge, planning for an imminent move back to the States, and an invitation to tea with a woman who writes notes on fine stationery, you are one busy "Watcher." I love the "Cambridge Student" stories you have heard from merchants. They sound like a Walter Winchell *On Broadway* column!

Emily Mayview—a name from your past. How uncanny that she is living in Washington State! I wonder whether your lives could become intertwined again. Probably wishful thinking on my part as you still don't know with any certainty where Thomas will take a position.

Bert assures me that he wrote to thank you for the lovely Onoto fountain pen. It was so thoughtful and generous of you to send something "English."

I took him to Thomas and Gassman last week to shop for school. He chose a camel's hair and a corduroy sports jacket. He was fitted for a pair of brown oxfords and a double-breasted camel's hair coat. A couple of shirts and slacks later and he was set for his first year. He is not hard on clothes and has several other items at home to include in his wardrobe. Thank goodness we had already bought a suit for his graduation!

Catherine was so deflated when I told her that you would not be joining us at the Lake. Our summers at the cottage are filled with memories of you and the girls being with us. We both are disappointed that you will not be with us at the Lake this year.

William is doing well with his studies; he is taking a summer school class and has found a copyboy job with the *Chicago Tribune*. The school and the *Trib* have worked together to provide positions for students who wish to apply. As long as he can keep up his grades, he will keep the job.

Seamstress Catherine has been staying busy this summer with babysitting and sewing. She has fashioned some very simple but colorful dresses for school. She has her own ideas about fashion and normally I don't say much to restrict her choices of fabric, but when she decided that she wanted to wear red and white striped socks with her plaid skirt, I drew the line. I've seen other teens her age wearing the same socks, but not my daughter! *Life* recently had an article on teenagers. One photo was of several girls wearing the very same knee-high socks. I wonder where Catherine's life will take her. She is such a blithe spirit.

Now that you are current on the family news, I will try to give you the latest in the continuing saga of Larry Blanchard's nurse friend, Carla Thompson. Larry considers himself very lucky to be out of the relationship. I concur. The Thompson woman has been the subject of front page news for weeks.

She was never charged with murder, but she was charged with drug fraud after obtaining more pills than she was prescribed. She claimed she had lost the original bottle of pills and had obtained a replacement prescription from a different doctor and different pharmacy—neither physician being Larry Blanchard, thank goodness! Carla pled guilty to drug fraud and was fined, but not jailed.

Several prescription drugs were found in the bodies of both of her former husbands, but embalming had limited the amount of medical evidence that could be found from the autopsies. She will not be charged with murder, although the families of both men have sent a petition to the Governor in the hope of having a special prosecutor appointed.

The whole situation is so ugly. We are just grateful that the Montrose Clinic wasn't dragged through the mud. Larry has taken some more time off; a good start to *really* healing, I hope. He is terribly lonely and was probably very flattered that Carla found him interesting and attractive. He and Karen have a daughter, Madeline, who is grown but who doesn't live here. Coming home from work with no one to share the day must be horrid for him. I've asked Julia to bake some extra sweets for him when she does our weekly baking. The scalidi will surely bring a smile to his face.

Julia is still tutoring a few students on Saturdays. Being able to have the children come to our home makes it much easier for her. But now that it's just the two of us left at home, I don't know whether I can keep her busy.

I do have an idea which is finally bubbling to the surface. I must say it could be something that will take

Larry's mind off his problems and one which could relieve me of worrying about Julia.

I am of the opinion that were we to build a new clinic, the old clinic could be used to house an innovative and most needed child care facility. The program would serve children of hospital workers as well as those we employ. Julia could most certainly serve as its directress. She has the education and knowledge. Larry has the experience of beginning a business from nothing and building it into successful entity. They'd make a great team.

During the war years, Kaiser had a wonderful child care center for its workers. I believe it to be a perfect model. On-site, affordable, education-based child care, perhaps even pre-cooked meals could be sent home with the family so parents don't have to cook. All for a price, of course.

Many women have had to leave the workforce since the war ended and the need for child care is less of an issue. But for those who are still working, medical care workers in particular, the issue is pressing.

I plan to present the idea to Larry when my vacation is over. But first, I want to spend some time outlining my proposal. I think that I need to have some specifics, or at the very least something written rather than just tossing the idea out and hoping that some of it sticks. It seems that I will have some quiet time, beginning tomorrow when Catherine and I leave for the cottage, to do just that.

I can hardly wait to hear your description of tea with Edith. Do keep in mind that you are *not* her inferior! "Class" should no longer be a part of your vocabulary when describing yourself. You soon will have your American citizenship. In the U.S. we are all equals!

With much love,
Margaret

August 29, 1948

Dear Margaret,

I was very happy to hear from you and relieved to hear that Larry Blanchard is still around. My imagination ran wild as I worried that he might have married Carla Thompson in haste and met with an untimely death as did her first two husbands.

I am relieved that his name, and with it the name of the Montrose Clinic, will not be dragged through such a scandal. How nice of you to provide him with Julia-created sweets. Is he making new friends? No doubt planning for the new clinic will keep him involved in life until he is ready to reach out once again. Has he met the scalidi creator? If not, I am sure that you have an introduction planned.

Your idea of a child care facility programmed on the Kaiser model could really help the community. Even though many women do not work outside the home, those who do need high quality care for their children. A good daycare facility will provide an incentive for health professionals to choose to work at Sacred Heart Hospital and other nearby medical facilities, particularly your clinic.

I know you are eager to read of my meeting with Edith Elizabeth Elliot. Upon receiving her letter, I wrote back directly and the answer came in the following day's post. She was most anxious that we meet. She invited me to join her for tea at the Ritz Hotel. I must tell you that the hotel is worthy of its name. I am rarely at sixes and sevens about what to wear but I must confess that I was in a dither on the morning of that day.

My girls took me in hand. They dressed me in my classic black dress and festooned me with a purple and red scarf, a broach that came from I know not where and red gloves. On my head they placed a red hat at what they called a "jaunty angle." I do not know how jaunty I looked when I came up to ground level at the Piccadilly tube station. I stopped, peered into the reflective glass of the hotel, and reseated my hat.

Not until I entered the lobby of the Ritz and found other women dressed in similar fashion, did I begin to relax. As I found my bearings and began to walk toward the tearoom I was intercepted by a woman about my height who was also dressed in a black frock much like mine and who was wearing a tasteful blue hat. Her effulgent greeting nearly knocked me over. I was grateful that my girls frequently run up to me with enthusiasm. Else I fear I would have fallen back.

I struggle to find the words to describe the expression on Edith Elizabeth's face as she met me. Perhaps members of the fire brigade receive such looks when they rescue a person from a burning building. Her face expressed joy and gratitude and relief all at once. She took my arm and led me steadily to the table she had reserved. I honestly do not know how to describe the hotel. Crystal chandeliers, linens, china, excellent food and service, and exquisite furniture all fused into an image of consummate luxury.

Edith Elizabeth herself is a lovely woman. Words gushed from her mouth as she acquainted me with her situation. Mrs. Beasley, our favorite grocer in Highgate would have said that the lady was in a "fair muddle." She began by describing her upbringing, her war work and her current position. While working in a dispensary, she met Dr. Martin Evans. Circumstances put them together every day and they soon became friends. Of course, she described how he was like no other man she had ever met. I assured her that I could relate because that is how I had felt when I met Thomas.

She had so much to say that I ate my savories, drank three cups of tea and had moved on to the scones before I could utter a word. Margaret, I will confess only to you that I don't think I would have had the heart to discourage her even if I had been less convinced of the wisdom of the match. Luckily, I did not have to make that choice. She described Martin as a good person, reputable and kind, who truly loved her. However, he had remained in England as long as he felt possible and was approaching the time when he would need to leave, with or without her.

She explained how in desperation, she contacted Susan Marchison, whom she had known since they were in Girl Guides together, and poured out the whole story. Susan responded that her neighbor in Highgate might possibly be willing to talk with her.

Once she paused for breath I was able to defeat her fears of the "wild west." I described Spokane and drew her a map of the State of Washington. She was glad that it was on the sea. I felt compelled to explain to her that the sea was actually quite far away. She was surprised to learn that the whole of England was smaller than Washington State and that it was further from Spokane to Seattle than from London to Land's End.

She was not discouraged in the least. Even the description that I gave her of your cross-state trip, the sagebrush in the center and the stark bluffs along the Columbia River did not dampen her enthusiasm. After all, I had lived there and was willing to go back and Agatha Christie had spent time in Egypt, living in archeological camps and loved the adventure.

Her beloved Martin had been offered a position at Kadlec Hospital in Richland, Washington, which according to his description, is one of the fastest growing areas in the country. I did remind her that you had found it somewhat dismal. She asked no more questions about that. She sees that part of the world as the land of opportunity.

She was mainly concerned with whether or not she, as a British woman, would be accepted. I was able to assure her on that subject. I described how my accent brought me instant friends. I also related that more than one person had said: "I could listen to you talk all day."

Before we parted we determined that Thomas should meet Martin and we arranged to meet again at a teahouse on Muswell Hill during the following weekend. The girls came with us and a good time was had by all. As we walked through the teahouse door two people greeted us with radiant smiles. Edith Elizabeth had accepted Martin's proposal.

The girls visited with us for a few minutes and then excused themselves to move to another table. Maemi then returned to our table and asked Edith Elizabeth to join them across the room for a brief discussion. As I watched the trio I noticed that the girls looked very concerned and serious as they explained something to Edith Elizabeth. They then returned to our table to discuss the problem.

The girls' concern was that Americans would not be able to handle the name Edith Elizabeth, let alone the moniker "Edith Elizabeth Elliott Evans." They had come up with a suggestion that once she was married and living in the U.S. she merely introduce herself as Forey Evans. It took me a few seconds to figure out that "Forey" came from her initials; E.E.E.E. I was shocked that they had proposed such a thing but she seemed to be considering their suggestion.

We returned home but not before Martin and Thomas had made a plan to meet again on Tuesday. Thomas returned from that meeting with the news that he had a strong inclination to apply to General Electric for a position in Richland. The newly formed Atomic Energy Commission is recruiting heavily. He believes that his background in journalism and his security clearance make him a viable candidate for a certain position.

The financial rewards could be considerable, particularly when compared to other jobs in journalism. I do not consider money to be of primary importance. However, returning to a place in Washington State that is only a three-hour drive from Spokane is a strong motivator. You and I would be able to continue our correspondence but also able to visit frequently.

I do know that you did not exaggerate when you described the place. Should we move there, I am afraid that you will, no doubt, be exposed to the dust and grit and flat terrain each time you visit. Maemi and Keiko, of course, look on it as a new adventure and are planning to ride the bus to Spokane for weekends with Catherine and plan for her to visit them in our new home.

I will keep you informed as this process moves forward. Whenever we appear in the U.S., I promise to be fully conscious rather than in a near coma as I was the last time I arrived from England.

Please send my love and best wishes to Catherine and William and especially to Bert as he begins his university career.

Much love,
Moira

September 15, 1948

Dearest Moira,

Love and best wishes have been delivered to the children. Catherine is researching bus schedules from Richland to Spokane and vice versa!

No "introduction" of Julia to Larry is necessary as he has spoken with her several times in my home. He knows her capabilities in the kitchen, but I doubt he has any idea of just how professionally bright she is! I'm not trying to be a matchmaker, but in retrospect they would be a great couple! At the moment I am just interested in steering him to consider her as a director for the child care facility I intend to propose to him.

I love the *Tale of* Forey! Your girls are very quick. What a wonderful nickname! I can imagine Edith's amusement in actually calling herself that! Perhaps "Edie" would be a good moniker and "Forey" only to her very good friends! I will call her Forey and smile every time I do as I recall her nickname's clever creators!

If Thomas applies for a position and is hired by General Electric, then you will already have a friend (Forey) in the area! That would certainly make the transition for both you and Edith, I mean, Forey, much easier!

I assume that Thomas' interest in GE means that Richland, since it is a government-owned town operated by General Electric, is indeed the town in which you are to put down roots. I don't know much about GE, but I just read an article in the paper that said that the company is looking for private investors who are interested in leasing commercial land from the government. Investors would have to build their own buildings, although the government would provide electrical and water connections free of charge!

Sometime in the past I read that Hanford was announcing funding for the construction of two new weapons reactors as well as additional research. I wonder whether this is the area in which Thomas would be involved; PR work to make the weapons reactors more palatable, that is. I doubt that the U.S. has much taste for more weapons and that the word alone can conjure up thoughts of, God forbid, another war! It would take someone like Thomas, who writes so well, to put the public's mind at rest. On the other hand, Hanford has created an entire city not to mention multiple jobs for the area. Who would be inclined to object to weapons production in light of so many new job opportunities?

I await news of the day of your departure from England. Perhaps you'll live with us temporarily or at least until Thomas gets settled. I am certain that if Thomas applies for the position with GE, that he will be hired; I just know it! Blast! Another thing for which I have to await news.

Bert is settled in school and I await his first letter. William, forever the "big brother," took delight in showing him the campus again! Julia stayed here with Catherine, whose first day of school went well, too! The only downside is the deafening quiet of our home!

While in Chicago, I decided to sell my parents' home. There are several repairs to be made before I can list it. William will check on the progress of the contractor I've hired. I hope to have it ready to show in the spring. By then the gardens will be in bloom. I suspect that the first and strongest interest is going to come from Northwestern University. It pains me to know that they will merely raze it and put up another University building. I'm including a photo of the house since you never actually saw it.

We were disappointed that you were not with us at the Lake. Though in retrospect, it really was too much to hope that you would be in Spokane in August. Our time at Newman Lake was wonderful. I spent many hours pleasure reading, a true luxury! One book I read that remains seared in my brain is the epistolary novel, *The Ides Of March* by Thornton Wilder. The author uses imaginary letters and documents to create a picture of this dramatic period of history and of one of its most interesting personalities. The thought crossed my mind that one of our children might someday take our letters and use them to create a novel. Ha!

Catherine took her sewing machine and continued her effort to create a fantasy wardrobe for school. She brought her collection of Frankie Laine records, and a tube of *Tussy's* latest "*Two-in-One*" lipstick (*Garden Party* at one end and *Midnight* at the other). She also brought a couple Judy Bolton mysteries. Unlike Nancy Drew, Judy ages in the books which seems to be something that Catherine is doing by leaps and bounds! She was good company for about a week and then I knew that she was getting bored with only me for company, so I allowed her to have a friend for a couple of days until Bert and William arrived.

Our only mishap during the entire four weeks was minor, but nonetheless frightening. We added a little Evinrude motor to our rowboat so our renters could get to the marina store without having to drive around the lake. All my children have learned how to use it safely. One day I allowed Catherine and her friend, Mary Kay, to take the boat to the marina across the lake from us. All was going well until they began the return trip. A storm came up very quickly and the boat began to fill with water; faster than they could bail. The girls were panicked and began screaming. Fortunately, their cries were heard by a nearby cottage owner who has a larger boat and motor. He was able to get them on his boat and tow ours to his beachfront before it sank.

As an aside, the rescuer, Douglas Linder, was spending his first week at his newly acquired cottage. He is an attorney who relocated to Spokane from Denver a year ago. He works for the County Prosecutor's Office. He appears to be our age or a bit older and is unmarried. After thanking him profusely, we exchanged phone numbers. I had fully intended to thank him properly by inviting him to dinner but the excitement of the boys' arrival and the activities that followed caused me to forget all about him.

Larry returns to work next month and among other things, I plan to bring up two items before he has a chance to sit down—the subject of a child care facility (even though there is bound to be a backlash from some who think that women should not be working outside their homes) and a new location for the clinic.

I should call Douglas, but I won't. I'm just too busy.

Love,
Margaret

September 28, 1948

Dearest Margaret,
I was so happy to hear from you and enjoyed hearing that Bert is adjusting well. I have always been impressed by how well the two brothers get along. William is definitely the oldest. However,

whenever there was a difficulty or a task to perform, they worked together beautifully.

The picture of your childhood home in your last letter makes it look even more beautiful and larger than I had visualized. I know that your parents chose the house in the expectation that my parents and I would join them. However, the coming of war and the sudden death of my parents prevented that plan from becoming reality. Just imagine the two of us playing on that huge porch and, years later, walking down those stairs on the arms of our suitors.

Even though the time has come to sell and you have not lived there for over 30 years, it must be a little sad for you. I am glad that William can handle the day-to-day business of the transaction. I think that Northwestern should make it into a faculty house with extra room for visiting professors. However, knowing how rapidly higher education in America is growing due to veterans using their G.I. Bill education benefits, I doubt that will be the case.

Thomas and I have discussed our Spokane house and have decided not to sell at this time. We shall continue to rent it and we are so grateful that you keep in contact with the rental manager and frequently cast an eye over the house while we are away. If we do indeed move to Richland, we can take a more active part in its upkeep.

Thomas is now heavily into negotiation with General Electric. One of the conditions he insists upon is that a house will be available to our family immediately upon arrival. I had thought that perhaps we could stay with you for a week or two of adjustment but he is most adamant that the girls get settled in school as soon as possible. I thought it a bold request to make to his potential employers but he insisted. We will visit you as soon as we are settled and very much look forward to your and Catherine's visit very soon.

The girls have returned to school and are working very hard. I am happy to report that Anna's brother, Ian, has not yet returned from the north and may never do so. It now seems likely that he will remain with his grandparents and help on the family farm. Even his mother feels that this is for the best. He could very likely be in line to take it over once they can no longer manage.

General Electric strives to recruit excellent employees in every field. In that attempt they offer well-built rental houses on curved streets which are about half the cost of houses in nearby towns. In addition, all utilities are provided. Coal for heating is included in the monthly fees and poured down the coal shoot in each house on a regular schedule. Electricity, water, sewer and trash pickup are also included. In addition, professional workers at Hanford earn 30 percent more than those who hold equivalent positions elsewhere.

From what you have written I fully realize that Richland is not the most aesthetic place on earth and I suspect that is why they go to such care and expense to attract a high quality workforce. Veterans who have recently finished college on the G.I. Bill and started a family must find such an offer nearly irresistible.

Maemi and Keiko are excited to begin reading the Judy Bolton mysteries. They have immersed themselves in Jane Austen novels and have nearly finished the last one. They are thrilled because all four of us have not only been invited to attend Forey's wedding but have been asked to stay in the family home. I am quite excited about that myself.

Forey describes it as a now-shabby gentleman farmer's house. Maemi and Keiko, who have both recently read *Pride and Prejudice*, screeched in unison: "Elizabeth Bennett's father was a gentleman farmer." I hardly think that we will be house guests in a carbon copy of Longbourn. However, should we be introduced to a friend of the bride named Charlotte, I fear that we shall all three screech in unison.

We received a very formal and gracious letter of invitation from Edith Elizabeth's mother, Mrs. Elliot. I must practice using Edith Elizabeth's proper name even though we have been calling her Forey since the girls created that nickname. Martin has mentioned that he looks forward to living in the U.S. where he will be able to introduce her to others as Forey Evans.

I suspect that we have been invited as houseguests because E.E. has talked of us rather a lot since she declared her intention to marry Martin, leave the country of her birth, and move to America. She has warned me that her mother is almost certain to look to me for assurance that an English woman can survive in the New World. Both of E.E.'s older sisters married men from neighboring estates and have settled nearly within walking distance of their family home.

No member of Martin's family will be here for the wedding so I suppose, since Thomas is an American, we will take their place. Thomas will be the best man and E.E.'s oldest sister will stand with her.

I am becoming rather excited about the festivities myself. I have been to very few proper weddings in England. My experience with marriage ceremonies actually comes from those held at St. John's

Cathedral in Spokane. There were a great many celebrated there while I was a member of the parish. I participated in a good number of them by serving at the reception, helping with the flowers, setting the altar, or as a guest.

Martin and Forey will be married, uncharacteristically, on a Tuesday. The date was chosen because it will be the first possible day after the three required readings of the banns (each on a subsequent Sunday) have been completed. The bride and groom will depart the following day, board a ship, and sail for America.

You can imagine the flurry in which we now live. We are sewing wedding clothes, giving the house a deep clean and packing non-essentials while trying to carry on the regular household routines of shopping, cooking, eating, washing up and tidying, which still take a few hours a day.

Now, my dear cousin, I must say something to you. Loathe as I am to issue you a command, I feel compelled to write two words: "Call Douglas!"

Much love from your cousin who wishes only the best for you.

Moira

October 14, 1948

Dearest Moira,

I wonder whether the GE negotiations are over and whether this letter will find you still on Talbot Road. You may never even read it!

This, I know for sure; the rental rate in Richland with the inclusion of all the utilities, plus a very generous salary makes the package fantastic! Since I have yet to receive a phone call from you, the only thing I know for certain is that you are not yet in the States. I have the feeling that General Electric has made its decision and that soon you will find yourselves living just a few hundred miles away from us. Catherine and I would love to be your first visitors!

I'm glad that you have decided to keep your home here as it is a lovely piece of property in a beautiful part of town. It is rentable and will be there for you should you determine to ever return to Spokane. Your property manager will continue to find renters who will care for your home as if it were their own. Hopefully, the family currently living there will not move any time soon. Nothing could be better than having a permanent renter!

Dr. Evans will be at Kadlec Hospital? That's wonderful! He will be a very busy man as just two years ago, Richland led the country in birth rate with 35 births per thousand compared to the national average of 20 per thousand.

Obviously, the area is bursting at the seams! As I understand things, Kadlec's services are no longer limited to only Hanford workers. I do recall talk of having such limited services and equipment at the original Richland Hospital that all emergencies and bed-patients were sent from Hanford to Lourdes Hospital in Pasco. I am certain that is not the case now. You will be well cared for. I believe there is a Medical Professional Building just across the street from the hospital. Perhaps that is where Dr. Evans will have his office.

I am enclosing a photo of Kadlec which I found in one of my journals. I hope the landscape doesn't dissuade you! The rambling barracks-like building is Kadlec.

Larry and I had a very long chat about a new location for the Clinic soon after he returned to work.

He seems strong and energetic, almost back to his healthy self. He feels strongly that we should stay within walking distance of Sacred Heart Hospital. Since our current facility belongs to him, I was certain that he would have difficulty leaving it. I was wrong! He was way ahead of me and already had plans for the purchase of property around the corner from our current location on Cowley Street. He also says he wants to go ahead with my plans to start a child care facility using the former clinic space to house the center. I know that he means he wants to "explore the idea," but I am confident that once he meets and listens to Julia's ideas, he will be a strong supporter.

Now for my big news: I am negotiating the purchase of a house on Harlan Boulevard. As crazy as this will seem to you, it is a dream come true for me.

Uncharacteristically, I have involved myself with a movie ploy, but after half of Spokane tramps through what I hope will be our home, perhaps we'll be able to forget the publicity and the hoopla.

The house is a promotion gimmick, the inspiration of a Hollywood producer named David O. Selznick. He encouraged contractors all over the U.S. to replicate the movie-set house that was built for *Mr. Blandings Builds His Dream House.* The movie stars Cary Grant and Myrna Loy. Seventy-three cities, including our own, are each constructing a "dream house." The house includes the latest atomic-age amenities: a mangle, a dishwasher and an automatic washer and dryer. It has been furnished by the Crescent Department Store and fortunately, my own treasures will fit nicely with those already in the house. It is absolutely lovely, but costs an arm and a leg, so I will never be able to retire! I forgot to mention that the most popular gadget is the automated garage door. One needs only to push a button, and up goes the door. I have included a photo of the house.

I know that you would be perturbed with me were you to learn that I have yet to call Douglas Linder. I didn't have to call him. He called me!

We then met one evening at Madge's Hedge House, which is just north of the Courthouse on Monroe. Douglas is very interesting. He's well-read, has a variety of hobbies including woodworking and tennis. When he asked me whether I played tennis, I was glad that I could say that I "played at it." We have a quasi-date on Saturday at Comstock Park to play a set or two. The match will happen only if the Indian summer continues. Both of us are so busy at the moment that I don't think either of us has time to start a relationship, though it was nice to play "dress-up" for an evening out!

I can hardly wait for you to get back on U.S. soil! I have missed you so!

Love,
Margaret

October 29, 1948

Dear Margaret,
I am writing you from London in a house at sixes and sevens. Only yesterday did we learn that we will indeed be moving to Richland. We pack while simultaneously trying to keep the house in good order for Eileen's imminent return. I am so glad that I placed my correspondence and letter writing materials in my valise. Else I may not have been able to find them. Carrying on a regular life while preparing to move is a challenge. I thank you for

your example. From you I learned much about organizing and managing a home, professional, social and church life. You made it look easy.

It pleases me to read that the plans for the Montrose Clinic and child care center are progressing in such a positive way. However, I admit that I was shocked to read of your search for a new home. What a surprise!! Here was I thinking that you were planning to move to a smaller house only to hear that you are purchasing an ultra modern movie house even larger than the one we all lived in together. I admire you for taking a chance and stepping out into the future. I should not have been surprised. You were one of only a few women to earn a medical degree in 1930 and continue to practice in what remains essentially a male profession.

Forey's wedding and our visit with her family was a once-in-a-lifetime experience for all four of us. Our prediction that her family home could have been the inspiration for a house in a Jane Austen novel proved true. Our first look at the symmetrical brick facade of the Georgian house nearly took our breath away. A perfectly centered pediment breaks the roofline above the entry. At ground level a "fan light" window above the massive doorway captured our attention as we approached the house on the perfectly straight path that led from the front gate to the massive entry door. The house loomed larger with each step we took. The girls nearly screamed, Thomas pumped his lungs full of air and I felt giddy.

The door opened as we approached. There stood the entire family. In the front rank were Forey and Martin, Forey's parents and her two sisters. A large number of people were crowded in behind them including children who jumped up and down to catch a glimpse of us. Such a reception I have never experienced. I half expected flashbulbs to flare and a crowd of reporters to assail us at any moment. Martin looked greatly relieved to see us. I imagine he felt as though his entire future depended upon our convincing Forey's father that his daughter would not be ruined by this strange marriage.

The tension was finally broken when children of all ages broke through the greeting party, grabbed Maemi and Keiko and disappeared down a long hallway and into the back garden. Our luggage was then whisked away and we were ushered into the house and through a doorway on our right into a large parlor, where a welcoming tea had been laid out in grand style. The most awkward moments of our entire visit took place directly after introductions were made and the tea was served. The room fell into a silence that seemed to last for four minutes, though I am sure it was less than a minute. Thankfully, Thomas began speaking. He thanked them for the invitation and described how anxiously we had awaited this visit.

His pronouncement broke the silence and general conversation broke out among the several groupings and continued constantly for around 90 minutes. We were seated with Forey's parents who asked a great many questions about the U.S. and told us how proud they were of Forey. They are, of course, sad and unprepared to see her move so far from home, particularly because she left the family earlier than they had expected to help in the war effort. Watching Forey interact with her sisters showed me that she is really quite a jolly girl—far different from the Edith Elizabeth I first met. I predict that she will enjoy life in the U.S.

The many hours we spent in the house between our arrival and the wedding allowed us to become fully aware of the toll that war had taken on the place. It had been used as a rest and rehabilitation facility for officers who had suffered immobilizing injuries. Soldiers who had lost one or more limbs, their sight or their hearing were cared for and rehabilitated for civilian life on these grounds.

It soon became obvious that the lounge where we had taken tea was the loveliest and best kept room in the house. The second large room, directly opposite, bore signs of having been subdivided into 12 cubicles. The well-proportioned dining room also showed evidence of hard wear. Scarred paneling marked the places where wheelchairs and other assistive devices had hit repeatedly and the wallpaper was stained in many areas. Above the ground floor, the first floor, which had accommodated the staff offices and a dormitory for the live-in employees, also showed signs of wear. The staircase that led from the ground floor to the second floor was scraped and scratched as well.

One modification, which the family has unsuccessfully petitioned the government to remove, was of great benefit to us. The military had added five large toilet stalls and five baths to the back of the house to accommodate the patients. Members of the Evans family see them as eyesores. We, however, appreciated them a great deal during our visit, particularly on the morning that we were all preparing for the wedding.

The ceremony was lovely, solemn and beautiful. Forey's relatives, close neighbors, the servants, and our family filled the pews. The bride shone with happiness as she walked to the altar on her father's arm. Mr. Elliot, however, bore the look of a brave warrior heading into battle.

We boarded the train for London directly upon leaving the wedding breakfast. The rail journey home to Highgate was a bit of a shock. The banging of doors, the yelling of the conductor, and the aged and dirty seats, brought me quickly back to reality. I have become accustomed to riding in old train cars with their gritty and torn upholstery but somehow, perhaps because we are preparing to leave, I really noticed the wear on this journey.

Your prospective new house sounds wonderful, especially the automatic garage door opener. Not needing to wrestle with the garage door while at the same time seeking shelter from the rain or snow will be a great boon. It will almost be like having a footman.

Perhaps it will be even better than having a footman. Forey's mother and I spent much time together during our four days in her home. She described her challenges in finding good household help in great detail. As a child she had enjoyed the family servants. It was only after she married that she realized the difficulties that come with managing them. Some had become unhappy in service and left and she struggled to keep the good ones in the family's employ.

She went on to describe the near impossibility of running a household during the war years and how she had looked forward to the post war years when life would return to normal. Of course, it has not. The male servants who had been called into the military returned anxious to find work that would allow them to live in their own rooms and not be on call at all times. The maids had left service to help with the war effort. Some had become Land Girls, others found work in factories, offices, banks and hospitals or joined the Women's Volunteer Services. Many married during and after the war. None were anxious to return to a life in service. Only the older servants stayed on and many of them were now becoming too old to continue the demanding work of running her household.

Mrs. Elliot was amazed that women no longer wanted to live in and complained that she has been reduced to hiring villagers to come in for day work. She has been forced into becoming her own head housekeeper. She also hinted about some financial woes that had befallen the family and voiced her concern that they would never be able to restore the house to its pre-war status.

Dear cousin, imagine me sitting and listening to her woes with a look of rapt attention. I am proud of the fact that I, who had virtually been a live-in servant myself for over 20 years, retained my equanimity, and neither smiled nor laughed out loud.

We are now organizing and packing as furiously as possible. It is hard to believe that we shall be away from here in less than a month. Thank you for sending the picture of Kadlec Hospital. Strangely, I read that it was named for the first person to die in the hospital, Lt. Col. Harry R. Kadlec. He was deputy area engineer and chief of the construction for the Army Corps of Engineers at Hanford, and it is said that he worked himself to death. I have never before heard of a hospital named for the first person to die there.

I must admit that thinking of the terrain around Richland does not fill me with undiluted joy. Nonetheless, I am glad to know what we will be facing. I now understand why the benefits of living in Richland are so generous. The search for workers is complicated even more by the fact that every single person working at Hanford or living in Richland must pass an investigation by the FBI.

However, attracting good employees is only the first hurdle. Those employees must also remain once they are hired. When the reactors were being built it was a considerable challenge to keep as many as 50,000 construction workers from leaving their well paying jobs. The high winds that blew frequently in that area were dubbed "Termination Winds." Once the ground vegetation had been removed from the building site, the bare ground took to the air every time they blew, causing many of the workers to "blow away" with it.

We will soon be living in a company town with few roads leading in and out, in a house not of our own choosing, with thousands of others in the same boat. Thomas assures me that we will be assigned a house that will more than meet the needs of our family.

I have learned that only a tiny proportion of women in Richland work outside the home. I must admit that I have quite enjoyed my work here as a Watcher. I was able to become an invisible presence and take note of my impressions of this, that, or whatever. There is very little chance that I will be able to do that type of work in Richland. Perhaps I can observe my neighbors and write about them.

Nonetheless, I am anxious to get there, set up our household and settle down. What I look forward to most, however, is living close to you and seeing you once again.

Much love,
Moira

November 23, 1948

Dearest Moira,

First, I must apologize for not answering your letter sooner. My thought was that my letter would only chase you around the world, eventually never reaching you at all. So I waited for a phone call saying that you, indeed, had arrived in the States and at last had a place to call your own.

It was wonderful to hear your voice, though the conversation was not nearly long enough! I am so looking forward to a lengthy description of your new home and actually seeing you in person. I am truly elated and certainly relieved to know that you are, at last, in Richland.

Catherine and I would love to come for a visit during the latter part of December. The boys will be home for a week before Christmas, but will return to Chicago on the 26th. We can come anytime after that. I am considering the train as that will allow us to get to you even if the roads are snowbound. Please don't hesitate to reconsider your invitation, should you feel not ready for company.

Your letter, albeit old news to you now, deserves my comment. The only home near Spokane that I know of with property and a manse the proportion of the Elliot's, now belongs to the Marr family.

Originally, the estate was a world-famous, thousand-acre cattle and dairy ranch owned by J. P. Graves. He called it "Waikiki," an odd name for a home in Washington State!

There are two tales as to how it received its name. One version is that after visiting Hawaii and thinking it "the most beautiful place on earth," Graves' son suggested they name their home, "Waikiki," as it was the second most beautiful place on earth. The other version is that JP, himself, named it "Waikiki," an Indian word meaning, "lots of rushing water." Since there are over 24 natural springs on the property, Graves thought it an appropriate name.

Your description of Forey's home, the family, and the entire visit was so vivid that I felt as if I were there as well. I can only imagine the visions that remain dancing in the heads of the girls! A "once in a lifetime" for them! You too, have had many experiences that will remain with you forever. A "live-in" servant indeed!

Now that the offer he made for the land on Cowley Street has been accepted, Larry is working with an architect planning for the new Montrose Clinic. I think the process may be a slow-go as there are so many concerns for which to plan and so much research to be done before we can actually break ground. At least we are moving forward!

Larry has met with Julia a couple of times during the past two weeks regarding the child care center. He is willing to convert the clinic's garage into a space that would house the center for the children of our clinic's employees. In this way, Julia could start out with a few children, while planning for a larger space to accommodate children whose parents work in nearby facilities. This too, cannot go forward until the conversion of the unused garage is complete. It will be a fanciful place for the children as there is room for an outdoor enclosed area in which to play. The structure itself is a wonderful blend of granite blocks and gingerbread trim. Another Heidi House, not unlike my own home, only much larger!

Larry, personally, has moved in a direction that I would never have predicted. He is preparing for the diaconate! Of course, this will take three to four years of study concurrent with his medical practice, but he seems in earnest and I certainly support him. I suppose we will soon be calling him Reverend Doctor Blanchard!

The only thing new in my life since last I wrote is a volunteer project in which I participated recently. Space in which to do breast cancer screenings has been allocated in the Paulsen Medical Building. There were three physicians and five Junior League volunteers in attendance the day I was present. Ten tumors were found, though all were determined to be non-cancerous. I was shocked by the number of women who came to the event. So many are, ordinarily, not able to get the screening for lack of funds. It's a very worthwhile endeavor and I intend to volunteer again next month.

Douglas and I have had lunch together a couple of times. He has met Catherine and she seems to approve of him. At the moment, he is involved with a high profile murder trial: a GI who shot his wife as well as two other family members. The service member is pleading not guilty by reason of insanity. He says that memories of the war caused him to think that he was back on the front lines. Douglas says that this is not the first time that an ex-military member has pled the same defense. It is interesting from a medical standpoint. Ira Levinson, the Clinic's psychiatrist, has seen two or three patients in recent years who have the same complaint. The defense also sounds vaguely like Julia's brother, John Seginni's diagnosis.

Your friend Emily Mayview lives in Ritzville, I believe? An article in the paper this morning said that there was an enormous fire in Ritzville that threatened the entire town. There had been high winds, which contributed to the destruction. Like Richland, the land in Ritzville is very flat. Although much of it is wheatland, there is not enough winter wheat to keep the dust from blowing around. The origin of the fire is unknown, but the new Trinity Methodist Church, which was just months from completion, was totally destroyed as were several nearby homes, the parsonage and a couple of other church buildings. I hope Emily and her family are unharmed.

I look forward to hearing from you soon. Give me a quick call once you get a phone installed so we can plan for Christmas! One thing I don't want to do just because we have phones to connect us, is to stop writing. Please do continue that!

This house was just too quiet! I acquiesced to Catherine's wish to have a pet. I suppose he will follow Julia around until Catherine gets home from school or perhaps he will even accompany Julia to the Center until the children begin coming. "He" is a darling schnauzer, salt and pepper, and so tiny that he fits in the palms of my hands. We have named him Vincent, after Vincent Van Gogh as one of his ears looks almost like no ear at all! At the moment there are many adjustments for all of us, but Vinny seems to have won everyone over with his sweet temperament.

All my love,
Margaret

December 3, 1948

My Dear, Dear Margaret,
Yours is the first personal letter delivered directly to our door. We are thrilled that you and Catherine will be our first visitors when you come on Boxing Day.

A new puppy? How wonderful! Welcome to the family, Vinny. I can only imagine how much Catherine dotes on your new family member. I love your choice of name too. I imagine that his feet seldom hit the floor when anyone else is in the house. We are most anxious to meet him.

There is much to show you and I have months of conversation stored up. I am glad that, along with our brief telephone calls we will also continue our written correspondence. Calling on long distance telephone lines is costly and I suspect that we will not do it frequently. Thomas has warned us that, if we do make long-distance calls, we must be certain to stay within the three-minute limit, after which the per-minute rate soars. It can't take more than a day or two for our letters to get to one another. However, I have been told to add an extra day on each end as the Richland Post Office is bulging at the seams. Adding to the time delay is the additional screening to which all mail coming in and out of the city may be subject.

Perhaps on our next visit to Spokane we will be able to drive by Waikiki, check on the clinic progress and see our old haunts. I hope to be able to talk with Larry. His becoming a deacon is wonderful news. His studies no doubt bring him solace and a way to deal with his loss. I am sure that he will be of great service to others who have experienced a similar tragedy.

I am reminded of the time when both my parents passed away within the same week. There was no counseling. I kept my upper lip stiff and proceeded on with my studies while my teachers swarmed about me to help. I was very sad but I did not feel deserted because the teachers at my school divided up to help with the tasks caused by the sudden death. They found me lodgings, took care of the family belongings, cleaned and vacated the house in which we lived, and helped me stay in school until I reached the "school leaving" age of 14.

I must have still been in shock when, as the school term ended, I was whisked away to the Mayview family where I was gradually and gently taught the skills necessary to become a mother's helper. I have no memory of the vicar or anyone else talking to me about my loss. Nonetheless, looking back, I realize that I was treated gently. I was not thrown into the world of orphans described by Charles Dickens in *Oliver Twist*. Perhaps I was treated gently because my father had been well loved in the village. No matter the reason, I am grateful.

I shall write Emily Mayview at her new address. I certainly hope the Ritzville fire did not impact her life. Since her husband's family was from this part of the state, perhaps she and her husband will pay us a visit later. They will not, however, be able to get anywhere near the former town of White Bluffs where he lived as a child. That area has become part of the nuclear reservation.

How can I describe the day we moved into our new house? We were driven to our home and dropped at the front door. For the first half hour each of us walked around like a cat exploring new territory. Upon opening the door, we saw before us a staircase leading directly to the second story. Turning left took us into the dining room with the kitchen beyond. A right turn led from the front door into a large parlor, pardon me, I mean living room. Just near the back door is a small room with a toilet and sink.

Upstairs we found four bedrooms and a bathroom with a toilet, vanity, and bathtub. The girls have already chosen their rooms, claiming the two middle-sized rooms for themselves. Thomas and I claimed the largest room, and the small one, which is about 7 by 10 feet, will serve as our guest room and work room. They insist that all three girls sleep in the same room during Catherine's visit, though I doubt how much "sleep" will actually occur. You will then have Keiko's room, which is really quite pleasant. The house is solidly built and completely furnished with pieces stamped *HEW* for Hanford Engineering Works. We discovered a half-basement, which contains a coal furnace, an area for clothes washing, a plumbed sink and extra space.

Before we had time to think about what we might need, the doorbell rang. First came neighbor, Blanche, who introduced herself, walked into the kitchen and plugged a percolator pre-filled with water and ground coffee into the outlet. She was out of the house in about three minutes. Next came another neighbor bearing a bottle of milk, a canister of sugar, and a plate of cookies. We four sat down immediately and heartily enjoyed our snack. All this happened before we even realized that we were exhausted and hungry.

A half hour later, Susanna arrived and departed just as quickly after depositing a casserole of noodles and cheese in our oven. As it warmed, a parade of neighbors marched in and out until our cupboards held a box of cereal for breakfast, several pieces of fruit, two loaves of bread, peanut butter and jelly and our refrigerator cooled two quarts of milk, a pound of butter, a pint of cream, a head of lettuce and four tomatoes.

We were both shocked and grateful. Around 7:00 that first evening, Forey and Martin came to visit. We told them of our extraordinary welcome and they explained that, in Richland, where everyone is a newcomer, this is standard operating procedure.

She pointed out the names that were written on a strip of tape affixed to the bottom of each casserole, the percolator, and the loaned dishes. Usually one of the neighbors was scheduled to drop by to give this orientation speech but, because they learned that we were friends, Forey was asked to welcome us. She told me that I would be invited to participate in many activities. I am grateful she forewarned me because I was quickly overwhelmed with opportunities.

As I returned the loaned kitchenware, I became acquainted with the generous women who had welcomed us. I made notes after each visit. The vast majority are between 20 and 30 years of age. Forey was correct. I have been invited to join a Bridge group, a Canasta group, and a Pinochle group. I have been presented with a list of available activities. The short list includes knitting, sewing, tatting, embroidery, quilt making and fashion design. There are also service projects, opportunities to help young mothers and schoolchildren. I simply cannot list them all. I thanked each neighbor for her invitation and replied that it would take me a bit of time to adjust and settle in before I chose my activities. I don't wonder that Forey returned to the working world almost immediately after she arrived.

I am being introduced as the English lady, a term I would apply to Forey but not to me. I am once again gobsmacked by all the attention. However, the same is not true for Maemi and Keiko. They approached their schools with great enthusiasm. During this first week, they have each tried out for a play and seem to be fitting into their routines immediately.

Now that I have had a few minutes to sit and think, it appears as though we have moved into a seemingly ideal world with much to recommend it.

Thomas is well compensated, housing is more than adequate and the girls have slipped into their new schedules without a hitch. The schools here are marvelous at accepting new pupils. New faces appear in classrooms every day.

It also pleases me no end that I am now within 150 miles and less than four hours from your house. I can find nothing specific about which to complain.

Returning to abundant groceries, a large refrigerator and this pleasant December weather all help my transition. I have also enjoyed ample time with Forey who shows no trace of adjustment problems. Perhaps it is partly due to her being a newlywed but I do not think that is the entire story. She thanked me for warning her that neighbors and co-workers would love to listen to her speak. I think she rather enjoys the attention.

And yet, I miss my occasional work as a Watcher and find myself doing it on my own time. While our town is not fenced, traffic into and out of Richland is carefully watched. Employees are bussed from bus stops in their neighborhood to their working areas. I was told of one worker who drove into town in a big fancy car and declared that he was going to race down to the plant at a high rate of speed. He was quite surprised when no policeman followed. However, when he came to the razor wire topped fence at the end road he was met by an impressive force of officers, vehicles and even an armored tank. Neither he nor his car was seen around Richland again.

Agents of the Federal Bureau of Investigation have a strong presence here. They live in Richland and their children attend the local schools. They pay a visit to each family at least annually to ask about the neighbors. They may be checking for spies but I think they are also interested in learning if Hanford employees or their family members are engaging in activities like infidelity, gambling, excessive drinking, or other vices that would leave the individual vulnerable to blackmail. Another notable difference in this town is that no one talks about what work is done by the family wage earner. It is simply not discussed.

When Thomas worked in England, I was aware that he was in possession of information that he could not share. I understood and it did not trouble me. Here, we wives are instructed not to ask anything about the work of our husbands. I have even been told that, should my husband begin to talk in his sleep, I was to move to another room.

It won't be long until we see each other and I can scarcely wait. Sightseeing will take very little time and we look forward to taking up every minute that you are here with one exception. We have promised Forey and Martin that they can meet you even if only for a few minutes. Martin is also most anxious to hear the particulars of the temporary breast cancer screening clinic in which you participated.

Give Catherine my very best and give Vinny a good cuddle, too.

Love,
Moira

December 14, 1948

Dearest Moira,

I am so very happy to know that you are getting settled and have time to entertain Catherine and me for a couple of days. I do hope Keiko won't mind giving up her room. I'd give anything to be a mouse in one of the corners of the room in which the three girls will be sleeping. I suspect they will be up until all hours of the night!

Julia will care for Vinny while we two are gone. She has even more work now than a couple of months ago when I was wondering how to keep her busy; lots of little muddy paw prints on the kitchen floor!

My first reaction to your letter was, "Are you serious? Move to another room should Thomas talk in his sleep?" You might have acquiesced to those instructions in another era, but certainly not in 1948! Surely, the FBI knows of *your* wartime clearance! Having your personal life under a microscope is a concept so foreign to me. I admire your determination not to allow it to overcome you. Being a submissive, docile wife in this day and age is positively medieval. Having said that, please be careful as you "watch." Who knows who is watching *you* as you are watching others?

A second thought along the same vein is one that you may consider when you are feeling settled. That is, that you return to paid employment. Why not? The girls are happily established in school. Thomas is gone most of the day. And you...well, you sound as if you might be just a wee bit bored. It's either work or a women's group of some sort. I wouldn't enjoy the latter, but you might until you decide otherwise. Personally, I think Forey has the right idea! Perhaps I could bring the gorgeous, uncompleted stole you were embroidering for the Bishop before you left for England. Since you are still in his diocese it wouldn't make a difference as to where you completed it. On the other hand, it sounds as if you have more than enough choices for interaction in the community so you may not even want to think of that project!

This tidbit may be of some interest to you. Larry tells me that initially there were only two churches in Richland, a Catholic Church and a Methodist Church. But in 1947, an Episcopal Church was formed with 42 charter members and Reverend Leo Dyson as the vicar of all four of the mission churches in Kennewick, Pasco and Prosser. He also said that many of the Dupont Management team were Episcopalians and wanted their own church rather than sharing with the Methodists.

Your new house sounds spacious and cozy at the same time. Could it be Cape Cod in style (my favorite next to Colonial)? Do you have eating space in the kitchen, or will you eat all of your meals in the dining room? I can only imagine the delight of all of you to finally have a house to call your own. You will soon make it a home. Have you need of any of the furniture that is in storage here? I would think you would want some of your own things.

I can hardly wait to see you. We will arrive on December 26 at 11:05 a.m. on the Northern Pacific North Coast Limited. We board in Spokane at six a.m., and will have time for breakfast and a short nap before arriving in Pasco. I realize that the 26th is a Sunday, but when making the reservations, I wasn't certain that Thomas could take time from work to meet us on a weekday. We can stay until the thirtieth as you suggested. We will make other arrangements to get to the station for the return trip.

We received disappointing news this week. Our bid on the house was not the winning one; in fact we were involved in a bidding war, which then became an auction! At any rate, the Rogers family, not the Walkers, will be living in *Mr. Blandings' Dream House*. Back to the drawing board, as they say. Not willing to stay down for long, I am now looking for property. After watching Larry work with an architect, I decided I could do the same thing. I have definite plans to downsize and you were correct when you said that the "movie house" was not going to give me that option.

A letter finally came from Sarah. She and Lloyd are living in a kibbutz in northern Israel. It is located to the south of the Sea of Galilee. They went to Degania Bet despite the Arab-Israeli War that is in progress. The fact that she is a nurse and he a physician made the choice logical, I suppose. I can't help but fear for them. Last May, Degania Bet and Degania Alef, kibbutzim near one another, halted a Syrian Army advance into the Jordan Valley. When and if peace ever comes to their land, Sarah and Lloyd will enjoy the almond orchards and the date and avocado plantations. Sarah's description of their lives and new homeland sounds chaotic at best, but she does describe the beauty of the land as she imagined it to be. If nothing else, she is very positive about the move despite being caught up in the struggle.

Douglas is joining us for Christmas Eve. He has yet to meet the boys and has expressed some anxiety which I find endearing. I will describe the encounter when I see you.

Merriest of Christmases!

With love,
Margaret
P.S. Perhaps we might have a second Christmas at your home? We could bring your gifts when we come. Not only would it start a new tradition, but it would save us from standing in line at the Post Office.

December 20, 1948

Dear Margaret,

We are so excited that we can scarcely breathe at the news of your Boxing Day arrival. We shall make it a second Christmas and none of us will need to send parcels. Have no fear about Keiko giving you her room. It was her idea, her insistence, really. I cannot imagine that any of the three girls will be able to sleep at all that first night. They have months of stories to share and, if the past is any indication, hours of giggling as well.

I hope that you are not too disappointed at being outbid on your movie house. I feel confident that everything will work out for you just as it should. By the time you get here you will be able to tell me all about your Christmas Eve with Douglas, Catherine, and the boys. It will be fresh in your mind when you arrive and I am ready to hear every detail. Perhaps now that both of them have embarked on their own lives it will be easier for them to accept Douglas—and perhaps not.

You will be happy to hear that our home is a colonial, your favorite style, very symmetrical with a central doorway and four windows on the front, two on each floor. I think you will like it.

Currently it is furnished with serviceable and sturdily built maple furniture. Our living room holds two side tables, two padded chairs and a settee with a back that can be laid straight down to create a sleeping area for visitors. We called them "put-you-ups" in England. A table and chairs fill the dining room. The kitchen holds the regular appliances but does not contain a second table. Each bedroom is furnished with a bed, nightstand and chest of drawers. During the war years, the provision of completely furnished houses was a powerful recruiting tool. The families who moved here from all parts of the nation could start a household immediately, Spartan though it may have been, until their personal possessions arrived. Earlier this year, all the Hanford Engineer Works (HEW) furniture went up for sale to Richland residents. The former occupants of this house bought all the pieces, which Thomas purchased in turn.

I do not brag when I tell you that we live in one of the newest and nicest houses in this town. Thomas was given a choice of dwellings and chose this one from a diagram and a description. I am now fully aware that we live in this large house despite the fact that our family size does not officially merit our having a four-bedroom dwelling. In fact, with two daughters who could share a room, we would most likely have been assigned a two-bedroom house. Apparently the conventions are not always followed.

Status here is interesting. The Ph.D. scientists are afforded the greatest prestige, followed by military personnel. I think our status may be related to Thomas' high security clearance and experience as a journalist. His skills are extremely desirable now that we have entered into a "Cold War" with Russia.

No one has said anything directly to me about the house we were assigned. I detected whispers when I participated in an embroidery group. As far as I could ascertain, two of the women were surprised when I told them where we lived. Of course, they would never say anything openly. I was amused by their clumsy attempt at deception. They tipped their heads together and whispered (quite audibly) while keeping their eyes on me. When I looked directly at them, they instantly sat up straight like children who had been "caught out" by the teacher and began talking about an entirely different subject.

English women are much more talented than Americans at this sort of thing. They can make scathing comments so properly that their victim may feel that she has been complimented. For example: an innocent statement such as "she chooses such *lovely* flowers," spoken with just the right inflection could mean those flowers are gaudy and pretentious and certainly planted in the wrong place.

Except for the lovely maple hutch, which I intend to keep, we will no doubt eventually sell the HEW furniture and bring our things from storage in Spokane. However, I am much relieved that we are able to do so at our leisure. Until this year, Richlanders were provided with all their housing needs. However, next year we shall be required to replace our own fuses, faucet washers, and broken windows. Water and electricity will continue to be furnished at no cost and the coal deliveries will continue.

I enjoy watching those deliveries. The truck stops at each house after which a great clanking begins as the chute is lowered from the truck, the metal door in each basement is unlatched and the chute secured. The nuggets of coal slide through into our bin, the chute is removed and the process repeated at the next house. Each morning, after removing the clinkers from the firebox, Thomas shovels fresh coal from the bin into the furnace.

Our half-basement remains empty but some of our neighbors have created a small bedroom/sitting room in their basements, often with a chair, a toy box and bookshelf atop a small carpet. When I inquire as to why they would choose to spend time underground, the invariable answer is: "you will understand when summer comes."

We shall call for you at the railway station and return you there in time for your departure. You may be surprised to learn that I now possess a U.S. driving license. I have not been behind the wheel of a vehicle since I drove Wills' lorry that was held together with bailing wire, twine, spare parts from a second lorry and whatever additional parts could be scrounged during that time of scarcity.

During the week I can use the car all day if I choose. Thomas, like all employees, is delivered to his work locations in a blue bus. When Thomas bought our car at the Studebaker dealership, he strongly encouraged me to practice and take the licensing test. I thought I might feel unsure behind the wheel. However, as soon as the wheels began to turn I was flooded with memories of the first time I moved the old lorry. It seemed like I was sitting still while the world rushed past me on both sides. You can believe me when I tell you that our Studebaker is much easier to drive than Wills'vehicle.

Please do bring the stole I began to embroider for the bishop. It will be the perfect piece to work on during the meetings of my embroidery club. Perhaps I will be able to present it to him when he visits our congregation.

We find All Saint's Episcopal Church a small, but quite comfortable congregation, with which to worship. It is certainly no disadvantage to us to know the Dupont Management Team. They find our little family very interesting with an English wife and two children of Japanese descent. The grange hall where we meet doesn't hold a candle to St. John's Cathedral but it can be pleasant when decorated with the exceptional flower displays created by talented gardeners and flower arrangers. We take it in turns with the Lutherans to decorate the altar on alternate weeks.

Be prepared to adjust your ears to regional accents from all over the United States. Living in Spokane I quickly understood the "broadcast American" accent spoken there. Here I sometimes feel as though I am climbing the Biblical Tower of Babel. I am improving but yet it takes me a few minutes to follow the conversation of a woman who hails from New Jersey or one from the deep south, for instance. I make the same trouble for others and I am often asked to repeat myself during the beginning of a conversation. I am learning to say something quite simple and predictable at first to allow them to adjust to my accent before I launch into any topic of consequence.

Your suggestion that I consider something other than keeping house is well taken. I have given it some thought. I certainly cannot do the type of work I did in London. There is no opportunity to disappear into a crowd or to descend into an underground train station here in Richland. Everything here is light and open and above the ground. Perhaps I could do the same type of work in a different way. My job there was to observe and detect the normal rhythm of life in a particular location, notice when that rhythm was disturbed and write a report.

Perhaps there is another way to do the same thing. We can discuss this in person very soon.

We are most anxious for your visit.

Much love,
Moira

January 4, 1949

Dearest Moira,

Our time with you was simply wonderful! Everything about our stay was perfect. The only thing that wasn't, was having to leave! You are so missed. I thought I was lonely when you were living in Highgate, but I think I am lonelier now; and you are only 150 miles away! I must find a way not to dwell on the fact that you and I are separated once again.

I am so thankful that you got your driver's license as it allowed us to see so much of your new home while Thomas was busy at work. I am amazed that you know your way around so well. You must have been exploring while the girls were in school!

Please give my regards to Forey and Martin. They are such a lovely couple! I so enjoyed visiting with both of them. I am hoping that they will be true to their promise to visit us in Spokane. Although it was very forward of me, I mentioned to Martin that should Forey require an OB specialist, she would be well-cared for here by one of our specialists. I also mentioned that I know several OBs to whom I could refer her in Seattle. I didn't want to insult the staff at Kadlec, but it is a rather small facility. Martin was so kind to give me a tour. They have the latest equipment but even that does not replace skilled hands!

I loved the floor plan of your home. I am now working on a blueprint for my own home with an architect who is in the same firm as the one who is drawing up the plans for the new clinic. Jason Ratliff seems to understand my needs and requests; it is quite a simple process at this point.

I have found a piece of property a block south of Hutton School on Scott Street. It is on the Southeast corner of the street and what will be the backyard will get the afternoon sun. The area is just being developed, thus there are only two other homes to the east of my property. The rest of the area is wooded. There is a large pond hidden in the woods several yards from my property-line. I'm told it is a lovely place to ice skate in the winter, especially when the neighbors get together and shovel it. In the spring and summer, it is home to water and woodland birds. I am at peace losing the house on Harlan Boulevard!

Please tell Cornelia that I made her "Lemon Bread" for a potluck at the office. I got raves! Of course, Larry teased me that Julia had made it, but it was actually I who did.

Douglas, Catherine, Mary Kay Anderson (a friend of Catherine's) and I went skiing at Mt. Spokane this past Saturday. As I told you, Douglas is very athletic and because of that I have to work to keep up with him. Not that I mind. It is great to be out in the fresh air. Catherine, surprisingly, enjoys the sport as well. *The Spokesman Review* began a sponsorship of a ski school a couple of years ago and she has now taken two lessons and has pronounced herself no longer a novice. Riblet Aerial Tramway Company of Spokane has long been a manufacturer of trams for mining operations. In 1946, the company converted an ore bucket mining tram into a chairlift for Mt. Spokane. Supposedly it is the first double chairlift in the world!

Love,
Margaret

January 12, 1949

Dear Margaret,

How wonderful to see you in person! I relished our time together and am so pleased that it will be but a few weeks until we spend Easter with you on April 17. I am quite delighted, and yet not surprised, by how many of our neighbors managed to "accidentally" meet you during your visit. Many remarked that we resemble one another, which pleases me no end.

My mind keeps returning to your vivid description of the day your sons met Douglas. I am not a bit surprised that they behaved in a gentlemanly manner and am amused by the skill with which those two confident young men extracted from Douglas his entire life and professional history. How proud you must be of them both. You are my example for piloting our girls into adulthood.

Forey was most grateful for your information. She is, of course, thrilled to be expecting a child and is researching American birthing practices and comparing them to those in England. Should she need special treatment she will certainly contact you for guidance. She is quite a practical girl and does not worry excessively about childbirth. She knows that it has been going on for generation beyond generation, many of them without any medical aid at all.

I am so pleased that you liked our house and am most anxious to learn more about the one you are creating with the help of your architect. The pond sounds lovely—almost magical. It will be beautiful during every season. I am anxious to see the property when we visit in April. I am amazed but not surprised that you are becoming a skier.

Imagine being hoisted up the hill on a lift and flying down!

Maemi made a wise choice when she chose to write a report on the history of Richland for a class project. She began the project with gusto and I had no idea of how much she had learned until she brought her corrected project home this week. Her research and the interviews have given me the answers to many of your questions. She also enjoys her work as a volunteer who helps orient new students to Columbia High School. I was surprised because she is a relative newcomer herself.

You remarked about how well-built the houses appear, despite the speed of the city's development. Maemi discovered that in 1943 the entire town had 300 inhabitants and by the end of 1945, it had become home to 25,000. You may actually know the Spokane architect G. Albin Pehrson, who was given less than 48 hours to decide whether or not to accept the project, and less than 90 days to complete the design of the entire community including streets, utilities, and commercial and residential building plans. He was given few guidelines other than the number of families to be accommodated and a budget limit.

When he agreed to take on the project he had three employees. He immediately hired 300 more. His completed plan was more elaborate than the army originally wanted. However, DuPont Corporation insisted that it was necessary to offer better than usual homes to lure highly skilled workers and engineers. The government had plans for a continuing mission at Hanford and wanted the town designed for a permanent population.

The lumber used to build the town was taken from a fine stand of Douglas firs left after a 1929 forest fire near Portland, Oregon. The floors in the single-family homes like ours have three-quarter-inch oak flooring. Cedar shake siding was used because it was not costly, readily available and durable.

Maemi also conducted interviews. During one, she discovered that, before the houses were landscaped, they were indistinguishable from one another and men often walked into their kitchen after a long day of work only to find a strange woman standing at the stove. The first families to settle here also remember the tremendous dust storms that defeated their early efforts at landscaping. They told Maemi how they repeatedly planted the seeds that were provided them and assured her that the winds that rattle us today are mere breezes in comparison. Maemi also learned that the streets are named for deceased Corps of Engineer officers. George Washington Way and Goethals Drive are the only two that I recognized.

She also interviewed a few Richlanders who came here to work during the construction phase of the nuclear plant. Those original employees had no idea of the purpose of the project. Maemi interviewed Bessie Miller who had been earning $20.00 a month as a secretary in Nebraska when she read that secretaries made $60.00 a month in a place called Hanford. She convinced Nora, her 18-year-old sister, to come along. Neither girl had been recruited but that didn't discourage Bessie from buying two one-way train tickets to Pasco. She and her sister stepped off the train, walked directly to the new arrivals desk in the station and were hired on the spot. They performed the most menial of secretarial tasks until their security clearances came through.

Bessie described the tens of thousands of men who streamed into the area. A national manpower shortage had been created by the number of men in uniform during the war and the fact that factories were running at full capacity. Some Hanford builders had recently been released from prison, some could not read and others were missing a limb. But they were all able to do some kind of work. The few men who brought families with them were accommodated in a trailer park, which had laundry rooms and served the families adequately. Life was calmer there than at the building camp where the single men lived.

The single workers were housed in huge dormitories, two men to a room. DuPont knew that they had to feed and entertain their construction workers well to keep them from hopping the next train out of town. Therefore they promised their workers as much food as they could eat. Every seat in each of the eight dining halls was filled by a hungry diner the second it was vacated. Food was served family style. The diner who took the last portion from the serving dish raised it into the air and a food server instantly replaced it with a full one.

Circuses, Big Band orchestras and wrestling tournaments are but a few examples of the entertainments that were provided in the enormous recreation hall every night. Baseball teams were formed and cheered on by major-league-sized audiences. The construction camp was rife with semi-controlled drinking, fighting and gambling. The main objective of law enforcement was to get the workers back on their feet and able to work the next day.

Women formed only a small percentage of the workforce. They were hired to process payroll, work in food service and as secretaries. Women lived in barracks located in a separate part of the compound behind barbed wire fencing. Guards manned the gates for the women's protection. Minority race workers also lived in a separate living area, as they did on other construction sites of that time. At its peak, the camp accommodated 40,000 workers, speaking with a multiplicity of accents.

Dear Cousin, I must write you about my thoughts, even at the risk of making this letter too long to read in one sitting. One of my most vivid childhood memories is overhearing a conversation between my parents when they thought I was asleep. My mother asked my father: "Do you think that Moira thinks too much?" He answered quickly and defensively: "Certainly not!" I sometimes think that she might have been right.

The girls are very happy here in Richland. They can walk anywhere in safety. There are no questionable neighborhoods and no industrial plants to pass as they walk to and from school. They can safely play outdoors at night. Yet, my mind is troubled.

Perhaps my mother was right when she said that I think too much. I am struck by the irony of my daughters, who are of Japanese descent, happily living here in the place where the plutonium for the bomb that fell on Nagasaki was manufactured. The front page of the August 14, 1945 edition of Richland's newspaper *The Villager* carrying the headline, "PEACE Our Bomb Clinched It," is proudly mounted behind glass and displayed in several public establishments here.

Not until President Truman revealed the existence of the Manhattan Project, did Richlanders learn the purpose of their work. Shortly thereafter, the mascot of Columbia High School, which Maemi now attends, was changed from the Beavers to the Bombers. The logo was changed to a stylized atomic mushroom cloud with a superimposed *R* monogram, the *R* standing for Richland. A dented practice bomb painted green and gold serves as Col-High's mascot.

I can understand Richlanders' pride at contributing to the war's end. However, having been on the ground with bombs falling nearby gives me a different perspective. "Atomic Frontier Days" are coming in a few months. I shall need to steel myself.

I am as happy as anyone that the war has ended but thoughts and images of such a bomb disturb me. I remember the terror I felt as bombs rained down overhead, the hours I spent reading, writing and sleeping in a Morrison Shelter and later running through the streets of London with German rockets flying overhead until I could run no more. I appreciate being able to ease my mind of such things by expressing them to you in writing.

I am sorry to tell you that I will not be able to give Cornelia the message about the lemon bread. She is gone! When I glanced through my front room window yesterday morning I noticed a maintenance truck parked on her lawn. No one has remarked upon her absence—not one neighbor, no one at the market and no one at yesterday's embroidery circle. When Thomas arrived home from work, I merely looked at him with raised eyebrows and nodded at the newly vacant house. He returned my nod. Not a word was spoken.

Cornelia was a person who asked an unusually high number of questions. I was taken aback when I first met her. She asked how Maemi and Keiko spelled their names. Then she asked if that was the usual spelling of those names. I answered that I did not actually know because they had been named before I met them. She began asking another question but I turned my attention to Mary, who was struggling with a difficult stitch.

We English rarely ask a question of a stranger. When we do, we always preface it with "pardon me." After living in the U.S., I am accustomed to being questioned. However, here in Richland few questions are asked, other than former locations. As newcomers, we were asked where we came from in a variety of regional accents: Where ya' from? Where ya' hail from? Where have you lived?

Because everyone is new, Richlanders exhibit an open and welcoming friendliness. Since no woman can visit her mother or shop with her sister, ersatz families are created on the spot. However, questions are never asked about work or past history. Cornelia was different. Now she is gone.

I miss you already and anxiously await your next letter.

Much love,
Moira
P.S. Catherine asked me about the small bottles of cider-like liquid sitting in boxes on a couple of the front porches in our neighborhood. She feared they might be filled with secret chemicals. I have since learned that they are delivered monthly to the front porches of certain workers to be filled with urine and quickly retrieved.

February 1, 1949

Dearest Moira,

I, too, thought you and I resembled one another a wee bit. Perhaps that will continue as we age. My glasses identify me as Margaret, but I imagine in a dim light we could pass for one another. Hmmmm!

Maemi is a born leader! I know you and Thomas are very proud of both of your girls. Were we closer, I could let Maemi know how proud we are of her volunteerism and her assertiveness! I'd also like to tell Keiko how glad I am that she is learning to speak Japanese. Just being able to count from one to ten is an accomplishment! I hope she continues working on her native language. How fortuitous it is that your mailman be of Japanese descent and his wife a former teacher!

Thank you and Maemi for the interesting history lesson on Richland! I don't know Mr. Pehrson personally, but I know of him. He designed the Greek Orthodox Church, the Paulsen Medical and Dental Building and Sacred Heart Nurses' School and its auditorium among other buildings in Spokane. He also has drawn the plans for several houses. One house you might recall is the Victor Dessert mission-style home on Rockwood Boulevard. It's the one that sits high above the street with an enormous lawn and landscaping which skirts around gigantic basalt outcroppings. I think Spokanites sometimes believe Kirtland Cutter to be the city's only architect, however Pehrson is well-respected and very busy; though his name is not bantered about as much as is Cutter's.

I read that all of the Heywood Wakefield hard rock maple furniture gracing your home and others in Richland was procured from Frederick and Nelson in Seattle on a priority contract that took the entire allotment from other dealers nationwide. I wonder what shoppers all over the country thought when they realized there was nothing to purchase.

Your hardwood floors rival any I have ever seen. I have heard talk about Richland's housing area as "Alphabet Soup." They say that the blueprint of each home was given a letter of the alphabet to designate its style. Which letter of the alphabet is your home?

Since Thomas had "nothing" to say about Cornelia's mysterious disappearance and only nodded in response to your "questioning" look at her vacant house, I suspect that he knows exactly what happened to the family...where they have gone, or, worse yet, where they have been sent. Perhaps he is still in the "secrecy" business? I suppose you must accept secrets and oaths and the like, but it does not mean that you must never question events in your neighborhood. Your skills of observation are already keenly honed. You can't help but be alert to changes around you.

In my opinion, learning about one's neighbors after moving into a new community is the natural thing to do. Living in a community where neighbors know nothing about one another other than their names is so odd. How is it possible to *not* talk about your work at days' end with your spouse or with your friends? I recall seeing a notice in one of the shops you and I visited which stated, "For security, 'freeze up' this winter." I forgot to mention the poster to you, but at the time I saw it I thought: *"This looks like a war poster."*

The specimen bottles left weekly on the front porches of some workers and monthly on the porches of others is also very odd. One would think that providing a sample would be done at Kadlec Hospital. Who is analyzing those samples? For what purpose? What you are telling me about urine samples does not match with the idyllic community in which you live: crime-less, tax and social problem free, excellent schools, a state-of-the-art hospital, attractive—not to mention—subsidized housing, plus furnishings.

Do you think that there is any chance that somehow someone is monitoring what you say inside the walls of your own home? Could your phone be tapped? Do you think your mail is read? I suppose if "Uncle Joe" could bug FDR, then GE could do the same to you.

Who owns the *Richland Villager*? Is the slant on the news merely what GE wants you to know? I wonder whether the journalists, too, are sworn to secrecy?

I don't think that any of us can "think too much." We grew up with our mothers telling us that, but frankly, the way that the world has been spinning for the last several years and the way life is changing so quickly, one can never stop thinking!

I doubt very much that there will be much to see of my new home when you come in April. We have had snowstorms for the last couple of days and more are expected. There is about two and a half feet of snow on the ground. The trains have been hard hit; some are running late by as much as 15 hours! Excavation for the basement took place, but then the snow fell and work has virtually stopped. I am still hoping that by New Years' Eve we will be able to welcome a new decade in our new home, though I don't relish the thought of moving in December.

Larry Blanchard will be assisting Bishop Cross at Easter Mass. He is thrilled at the prospect. By the way, he is so much "healthier" than he was last fall. He and Julia have been keeping company and both seem happy with the arrangement. They meet weekly to plan the Child Care Center. On the weekends, they have been together for dinner or the Philharmonic.

I wonder what you and Thomas will think of Douglas. At the moment he is in the middle of an ugly murder trial. Yesterday was the first day of testimony.

Every woman in the courtroom left, as the description of the crime was so grisly. The jurors' names were published in the paper, so I know that there was one woman on the jury. Poor thing! Douglas sees the seamier side of life at times, but he is somehow able to compartmentalize. He rarely discusses work, not because he can't, but because he sees no need.

My friend, Dorothy Darby Smith, is now giving speech and drama lessons in her home. Catherine has begged me to allow her to study with her. I spoke with Dorothy and she accepted Catherine as a student. She didn't interview Catherine, but has seen her perform in Children's Theatre productions. I have yet to tell Catherine and am keeping it a secret until her birthday in April.

Bert and William are doing well and are very involved with their studies. Bert talks incessantly about a recent graduate of Northwestern Medical School, whose name is Ralph Paffenbarger. The latter spoke to undergraduates recently about medical school. He apparently has gone on to Johns Hopkins University for his PhD. in epidemiology. Bert wants to follow in his footsteps. Apparently, Dr. Paffenbarger has an interest in polio and has been doing research with a Dr. Jonas Salk to create an effective vaccine against the disease. Is there any reason that Bert would not be hooked?

The boys plan to be home for Easter Break; but only for a few days. William can take only a little time from his studies and his work at the *Tribune*. He's still just a copyboy, but since February of last year when WGN (World's Greatest Newspaper) Television, owned by the *Trib,* began test broadcasts and then in April began regular programming, William has been spending any free time he has watching what is happening in the studio. The station operates from the Tribune Tower, which is also home to the newspaper. That, in itself, makes it easy for him to get to their floor. I don't know where his journalistic interests will take him, but the sudden interest in television may be a clue!

I do know that it will be wonderful to have a full house again and especially to have *all* of us together. I am anxious for you both to be able to see your friends, so if you can tell me who you would like to see, I will plan a get-together and invite all of them for one of the evenings you are here.

I encourage you to keep a journal of your observations. Unless someone is secretly filming your movements inside your home, or is searching your home when you are not present, and unless someone can find that journal, your thoughts and observations are safe!

Please take care of yourself! I say this tongue in cheek and not to frighten you: do not eat anything that comes from the ground nearby! I have heard that Hanford is manufacturing high-powered airplane fuel. Another rumor floating around is that it is creating some kind of chemical. Grow only flowers! Something noxious could be going up those stacks!

With much love,
Margaret

February 11, 1949

Dearest Margaret,

I was so happy to receive your letter. Life here is so frenetic some days that I forget who I am. Your letters bring me back to myself.

We all look forward to being together again as a family and meeting Douglas. From your description I predict that he and Thomas will get along like a

house on fire. They both seem to enjoy the moment and do not bring the ugly parts of their work into the rest of their days. I sometimes marvel at how much Thomas and I have to discuss even though we never speak of his work. I suppose it has been this way since we met in London when we were both engaged in work that we could not share.

Would it be convenient for us to arrive on the Thursday before Easter? We rarely take the girls out of school but they are so very anxious to visit with you and Catherine and their friends. We will, however, need to be home in time for them to return to school on the Monday after Easter. We assume that we will see Larry and, of course, get to know Julia. We do not wish to cause you a great deal of trouble but we would very much enjoy an opportunity to visit with our friends. A list of people we would like to see is included with this letter. Also, I would love to talk with Grace once again. She is so witty, artistic and lively. Untypically for an American, she can describe a person with razor sharp accuracy in very few words. I would enjoy an opportunity to give her a description of Richland and listen to her unguarded comments.

You no doubt remember meeting Betty Bayswater during your visit. She may have been introduced to you as "Bustling Betty." I have decided to join her newly formed group, the purpose of which is to create linens to be sold at a craft booth during Atomic Frontier Days, which will begin on August 11. You should consider joining us here; it will be very hot but should be an unforgettable event with a parade, crowning of royalty, rodeo, county fair and a celebration of the nuclear industry all rolled into one.

Our new group will create table sets to benefit the Red Cross. We will cut tablecloths and napkins from bold prints and plain fabric, and finish them with a machine hem. Later we will tie them with ribbon. Betty's group is unique in that we will work as individuals and meet only to choose fabrics. I am thrilled to join this productive group. We are all women who like to see tasks get finished. I predict that we will all gain satisfaction from watching the stack of table sets grow in our half basements.

This will allow me to withdraw from my embroidery group with impunity. I do enjoy embroidery but prefer to do it on my own time. While my hands are at work on the detail, my mind likes to imagine and think and puzzle out problems. Talking with others as I do needlework is not easy for me and is certainly no benefit to the vestment I am near finishing for Bishop Cross. Distracted by surrounding conversations, my mind wanders and my fingers follow.

Our house is an "L" house, one of the largest in the alphabet soup lineup. Since our family is quite small for such a house, we were asked to host new couples for a week or a fortnight until housing becomes available for them. We have recently hosted two couples and I found myself in the position of orienting newcomers to Richland. I was amazed to be considered an old timer but, in fact, after the first month we are all old timers here. What a contrast to England where families who have lived in a village for only two generations are considered newcomers.

Lilly and Kathleen, the female halves of the couples who stayed with us, each asked me a million questions. In addition to being new to Richland, they had both been married for less than a year. They expressed so much gratitude that I am beginning to feel like I have become an expert on both wifeliness and Richland.

Many of their questions revolved around food and, believe me, I am no expert on American food, particularly the omnipresent product named *Jello*, which is called *jelly*, in England. Here in Richland, it is used in recipes of every possible description. Bustling Betty raved about a salad made by encasing Greek olives in lime Jello and topping it with feta cheese. I was given a recipe for Hungarian Salami Goulash that involved simmering a jar of sweet and sour cabbage with salami, onions, and canned potatoes, cooling the mixture and immersing it in Jello. I must admit that I find these cold dishes barely palatable.

However, I frequently bring a trifle made with fruit, jelly (*Jello*), cubed cake and whipped sweetened cream to potluck dinners. Both of our mothers made this dish frequently in England and I imagine your mother continued to do so here in America.

Thank you for the perspective on our mothers' perceptions of our thinking habits. You, of all people know how my mind works. I always try to sort out and categorize concepts so that I can recognize and deal with them. Once I had the role of a middle class housewife all sorted out, my mind started working on other topics—like the types of women living here, the parts of the country that they come from, their socio-economic status and their personality types. I found myself trying to quantify how many women could fit into a category named "Southern Baptists with artistic tendencies, short fingernails and three children" and cross referencing them with "New

England Presbyterians." So you can see what a state my mind was in.

I must have telegraphed my feelings of frustration to Thomas without saying a word because yesterday he showed up unexpectedly at lunchtime. He announced that he had taken time off to greet the girls after school because he was quite sure that I would like to go to his place of work for an interview. He had heard of a position at the plant which he was certain would interest me and had arranged a meeting. It took nearly a half-hour for him to explain the situation.

Forty minutes after Thomas arrived, I was on the way to talk with an interviewer with an official letter tucked into my handbag. As I approached the appointed meeting place, a huge wave of relief washed over me. All my pent up frustrations and minor irritations began to melt away. I rolled down the driver's side window, threw open the wing window and let the fresh air rush over my face. I must admit, however, that here in Richland opening the windows in February is not as dramatic as it would be in Spokane where such action may cause a buildup of ice on the inside of the windscreen—I mean windshield. As you have noticed, when excited I revert to England speak.

I must have done well at the interview because next week I will begin working four hours a day, from 10:00 to 2:00 performing clerical tasks. My assignment is apt to change as additional security clearances come through.

I hope all is well with you.

Give my love to Catherine and, of course, pat Vinny for me.

Love,
Moira

March 2, 1949

Dearest Moira,

Of course, you may arrive on Thursday. We'll have an early dinner if you must leave on Easter Sunday. I think Mass is at 11 a.m. and we'll eat afterwards. I'm so glad we'll be together for the weekend. I'm certain that the girls will do fine without my making special plans for them.

How quickly your life has changed! I am so pleased that you have found employment. I want to jump up and down and shout "Hooray!" Living a "non-fiction" life suits you much better! You can only embroider so many pieces! Bustling Betty's group will help you maintain a pulse on the community and participate in an activity you enjoy.

I would imagine that the clerical work you did during the war years has changed drastically in five years. Maybe you'll be using an IBM Executive Electric typewriter? The clinic bought two just this past week. I'm unclear as to the scope of your work, but since you mentioned "security clearances," I assume it will not be just the run-of-the-mill, "type and file."

My work has been at a pace faster than I really like. Consequently, my workday seems longer. I don't mind the work, but I do worry that Catherine is being neglected. Julia is at the house when Catherine arrives home, but she is often out in the evening with Larry, leaving Catherine by herself. The latter is fully capable of being left on her own. She is very busy with school activities, homework and Dasidrian. She seems perfectly happy listening to music or reading in her room. I just don't like the idea of leaving her alone. Her brothers didn't experience that, though they probably wish they had had such independence.

I am so glad that Julia has been keeping company with Larry. Her brother John was recently found dead outside the hospital wing at Medical Lake where he was supposed to be kept under security lock. The temperatures have been sub-zero. He did not survive the exposure and no one seems to know how he got away or for how long he was gone. It's a black eye for the Institution and one which they don't need.

Do you recall my telling you of Bill Morgan? I met him while I was at a meeting in Chicago last year. He is a plastic surgeon who teaches at Harvard. I received a letter from him recently. The great news is that he is engaged! I'm very happy for him. The bad news is that a classmate of his, Jim Braden, a dental professor at the University of Rochester, was recently fired from his research position. I met Jim and his wife coincidently when I met Bill. The Bradens had been in Chicago for a dental meeting the same week as our meeting. I'm sorry to hear of their troubles.

The whole truth about the "bad" news about which Bill told me revolves around a 1948 study published in the *Journal of American Dentistry*. It was subsequently censored by the Atomic Energy Commission in the name of "national security." The evidence points to adverse health effects from fluoride in public drinking water. The study was done at the University of Rochester where Jim Braden taught. Fluoride and plutonium would be a very bad combination if they were to be dumped by Hanford into the Columbia River! I don't know whether his dismissal had anything to do with this study or whether he was even a part of it. But it begs the question, "From where do we get our water?"

Following on the heels of the Jim Braden story is my very strange week. I have yet to report my concerns to Larry or any of my other peers. Having said that, I delivered four babies this past week. One was perfectly healthy, one was stillborn, another terribly deformed and lived only hours and the fourth was a mongoloid. Of the last three, one mother is from Rosalia, one is from Colfax and the third is from St. John. All towns are south of Spokane in the middle of the Palouse. All families raise wheat. Their homes are within 50 miles of one another, but I do not know whether they have ever met. I have delivered babies with severe deformities, but those deliveries are few and far between. Three in one week is very unusual, especially because the families all live in the same geographic region. I am greatly bothered.

I have no way of knowing what other doctors are seeing in their practices but I intend to inquire. I'd like to ask your friend, Martin Evans, without raising any red flags or having Thomas fired. Perhaps it would be wiser to just find someone in Kennewick or Pasco …maybe at the State Meeting I can corner some acquaintances from different parts of the state and can learn something!

Joe and Delores Parsons were here for a weekend. They brought me up-to-date on the condition of their son who has been undergoing thymus irradiation with apparently good results. Therapeutic radiation is the standard protocol for his condition. It's amazing that in this case, irradiation can be a cure rather than a killer!

William will be celebrating his 21st birthday next week! I cannot believe it! What's even more impossible to believe is that he will graduate next year! He once talked of nothing but becoming one of Murrow's "boys," recalling all the radio news broadcasts he listened to as a child. I will admit that he has a way with words and is able to paint pictures with them, but as of late, I don't think that he is going to go in that direction. He has television in his sights!

Bert tells me he is very excited to be able to come home for Easter no matter how short his stay will be. He is looking forward to seeing all of us. I'm sure he will regale us with his stories of books he has read and information he has learned. He *loves* school. Sometimes I think he will follow in the footsteps of his professorial grandfather as he loves sharing his knowledge.

I have waited until the very end of my letter to tell you this news. I don't want to you to feel upset for me. I'm really okay. Perhaps I might be a bit sad thinking about what might have been, but "thinking" about it would just be a waste of time and energy.

Douglas and I are no longer seeing one another. We had a very civil parting over the weekend. He said that he didn't see our relationship growing into something more. He also mentioned, "You never seem to have time for me." I suppose that is true. My life is just too full, at the moment. I can't blame him; he always seemed to make time for me.

I'm sorry that you and Thomas will not have the pleasure of meeting him. You would have enjoyed one another, I think. I have not yet told the boys, but Catherine knows. She acted predictably...melodrama written all over her face. I think she rather enjoyed Douglas. He treated her as an equal and brought out her best qualities. I suppose I will not be able to avoid him this summer while at the Lake. We're bound to meet at the marina or store. I hope we shall always remain friends.

Please don't dwell on my loss. We had a wonderful time together and I have many happy memories. Douglas brought me back into the world of the living and I shall be forever grateful.

With much love,
Margaret

March 13, 1949

Dear Margaret,

I can scarcely wait until we arrive in Spokane to celebrate Easter. How comforting to live within a days' drive of your front door. Seeing Bert again will be fantastic! Thomas is especially excited to see him. He thinks of him and William almost as his own sons. William will be voting later this year? Unbelievable! His becoming a voter and choosing a career nearly brings a tear to my eye. We shall one day sit in our living room and watch him read the news on television. One of our neighbors, who hails from New York City, reports that her family receives television signals in their home for three hours every day of the week. Imagine!

The tragic death of John Seginni pulls at my heart. The number of those killed and injured during the war is nearly impossible to believe. Yet it does not seem to represent the actual human cost of the war. Those like John who returned healthy in body, but not in mind, are not considered casualties of that terrible time. Julia did all that she could for her brother. It must be a very difficult time for her. I am sure that Larry will be a great help as she recovers from her loss. Am I right in assuming that she also is a member of the Episcopal Church?

I remember Bill Morgan very well. I was very nearly convinced that you were going to propose to him at first sight. As to his information, I know little about the effects of fluoride but I do wonder why a medical study would be squelched in the name of "national security." I am sure that it could be possible that some of the Columbia River water used to cool the plant could have become radioactive. These reactions are so recent that little is known. I would not like to think that it caused deformities in newborns and yet, three children in near proximity and close to the same time does make one wonder. I shall talk with Martin privately and give him your address.

I am very pleased to hear that the Parsons' son is doing well. Treating him with radiation seems ironic, does it not? An American expression, that I do not really understand, comes to mind: "a hair of the dog that bit you."

What can I say about Douglas? He sounds like the kind of man who wants a woman to be at hand whenever he has time for her. On the other hand, he did give you a new lease on life and for that I am grateful. It may have been hard for Thomas to see his brother's wife with another man. I think he has now reconciled himself to the concept.

I enjoy visiting with Forey whenever we can find time. She and Martin nearly always work the same shifts, which is a good thing for a newly married couple. Thomas and I worked the same shifts in London, even though he was sometimes away. Until we moved to Richland, I never thought about the numbers of people who work through the night.

I am happy to help Forey adjust to America. One thing that bothered her was that Americans ask her many questions about her own background but reveal very little about themselves. She sometimes felt like she was delivering a lecture on the subject of life in England. She is curious about the different parts of the country and the lives of Americans and would love to learn about the regional differences in the United Sates.

I had to think a bit before I could help her. When I arrived in this country I was not thrown into the culture as was she. As I slowly emerged from my wartime trauma, you, Catherine, Bert, William, Maemi and Keiko were there to answer my questions. You gradually introduced me to others.

Here Forey is regarded as merely one newcomer among a community of newcomers. We live in this artificially created town of people who are all about the same age with many, many children and very few aunts, uncles, or grandparents.

I was able to explain to her that we "proper" English people are absolutely terrified of causing embarrassment. Therefore, we never ask a question that might possibly cause someone else to feel ill at ease. I assured her that Americans are not so easily embarrassed and most are happy to talk about their backgrounds. I advised her to ask a simple innocuous question of someone and predicted that she would be surprised by their willingness to talk.

She took my advice and was overwhelmed by a torrent of information. Using a large U.S. map, she has marked out the regions. She has also constructed a chart on which she lists local customs, foods eaten and expressions and idioms used in the various regions of the country. She is an ardent student of Americanism.

She credits me for helping her adjust to this new country. Her effusive praise makes me appreciate you even more. Not only did you keep me alive physically after I arrived at your home but you eased me gently into a completely new culture without my realizing it.

In a minor way, Richland, by pulling people away from their kin to all parts of the country, is creating a new kind of America. Traditionally, people do as their parents did before them. Here there are many more choices.

Maemi and Keiko have been telling me the story of the Oregon Trail—the 2,000 mile trek made across this continent by trains of families in wagons. Men drove the wagons on the trail, devised routes, found ways to cross streams and rivers and hills and hunt game while constantly on the watch for danger. Women cooked over campfires after full days spent walking and caring for children and animals. Temporary families were formed on those five-month journeys.

In a way, we Richlanders form families too. Children soon learn which house to run to when they skin their knee. In our area, it is Mrs. Able who puts Mercurochrome and a Band-Aid on the injury. If they have greater problems than she can handle, she walks or carries the injured child home. Mrs. Marchisini is always good for a sweet treat and a cold glass of water, and Mrs. Brown, who bears a startling resemblance to the games mistress of the girls school I attended, organizes the children into softball games and contests.

If you are not seated, please take a chair before you read this paragraph. This letter was begun over a week ago. I have just today returned home. The four-hour-a-day part time position that I expected to slip into gradually never materialized. On my first day of work, I was escorted into the bowels of a concrete building to meet with a man referred to only as Marvin.

After a long wait I was issued into an area that was in a great uproar. Marvin had disappeared. He was not in the Hanford Works, Richland, or apparently anywhere else in the entire country. I wonder if he was a spy. Could he now be in Russia?

I was immediately sent away to become oriented to my new position. Would you believe that I have spent nearly the entire past week in Maryland and New York? First, I spent time at Aberdeen Proving Grounds to become acquainted with ENIAC, an electromechanical machine with tremendous computing power. Its full name is Electronic Numerical Integrator And Computer. I can only imagine how much ENIAC could have facilitated my wartime sorting tasks.

Security was high at the Proving Grounds but it was just the opposite at my second stop, which was in New York City to visit the IBM Selective Sequence Electronic Calculator (SSEC). It was built in a former shoe store on the ground floor of a building near IBM's headquarters at 590 Madison Avenue. Three sides of the room held the calculator. The fourth was a large plate glass window through which people could watch it operate. I never did get used to being observed by the passersby. I imagine they mistook me for an expert, which amused me very much.

It is not long now until we can talk in person. We are all so very excited.

Love,
Moira

April 28, 1949

Dearest Moira,

First things first… Easter was wonderful! It is so good to once again be able to celebrate holidays with family! Secondly, these wishes come a bit early and I will phone you on your special day, but, *Happy Birthday*! I hope it is a lovely day and that all your birthday wishes come true!

I am still in awe of the many things that have happened to you in the last few weeks. Suffice it to say, I am not the least bit surprised that you now find yourself at the top of the Hanford heap, working with computers. Given the opportunity, you might have been creating the beasts, rather than just using them to perform your work tasks. The photos I've seen of the IBM calculator remind me of some gigantic telephone switchboard.

I'm not even going to pretend to understand the capabilities of the ENIAC and the SSEC. However, I am also not about to hide my pride in your accomplishments. It does infuriate me to be unable to shout the news to everyone here who knows you and to even those who don't.

Do you have any more information about "Marvin?" Is "Marvin" really his name? Is it possible that he just wandered off and died in the middle of the reservation? Perhaps he went the way of Cornelia!

My image of him is that of a character in some spy novel. How much information could he have taken? Your story could be the reverse of Igor Gouzenko's in *The Iron Curtain.*

I wish I could have talked to you at length about what *you* are really doing with those computers. It's probably something of which you cannot speak. I could tell by your body language, that it was a subject to be discussed only at *your* discretion or maybe not at all!

Could any of this intrigue put you in danger? I wonder what might have happened had you actually met Marvin in that concrete building.

I received a phone call from Martin Evans. We had a brief conversation regarding the births I described to you. He has yet to see any compromised deliveries since arriving in Richland, but agreed to quietly make inquiries. I can only pray that what I saw was an anomaly. Thank you for contacting him.

I hope that we can get together with the Evans' at the Lake this summer. I will inquire about the rental two doors down from Gillian and David. If it is available, perhaps the owners would be interested in renting it for a couple of weeks. What fun to have our two families—theirs and David and Gillian all in residence at the same time!

The framers have begun working in earnest on our house. The weather has been cooperating so they are making good progress. We can walk through and actually see where the rooms will be. The upstairs is still open and not the safest place to be as the sub-flooring has yet to be laid; Catherine and I did not venture there.

We met one of our neighbors-to-be while wandering about the property. Her name is Marianne Cottrell. She recently retired from the University of Washington after 25 years as a professor in Public Health Nursing. Marianne has never married and, the weekend we met, was being visited by her brother, James, who is also a professor at the University of Washington.

Marianne was well acquainted with Elizabeth Sterling Soule, who I recently met at one of the State meetings. The latter has become known as the "Mother of Nursing" in the Pacific Northwest. Elizabeth organized the Department of Nursing at the University of Washington which, under her direction, became one of the first in the country to be accredited in Public Health Nursing.

The Cottrells seem like very nice people and yet there is "something" about them. I can't explain why I say that, but our conversation was somewhat unnerving. James spoke about his career sometimes in the present tense and then he would abruptly switch to the past tense. Marianne did not correct him. As a matter of fact, she attempted to change the subject altogether. Pleasant, but "odd ducks," both of them!

The ground for the new clinic was broken this week. Progress will take much longer than that of a house, of course. After listening for a couple of years to the rumble of the construction of Sacred Heart's South Center and Southeast wings, we have become accustomed to the noise. Now we will be the cause of the cacophony!

I am somewhat concerned that our construction will be slowed by the Carpenters' Union which has recently refused to work for companies paying less than $2.20 an hour. That, coupled with the layoffs at the Trentwood Metals plant because of a business slump and a severe winter, may also slow down the construction of the clinic.

Larry doesn't seem to be devoting as much attention to the project as I think he should. He recently told me that he would much rather be involved with the diaconate than the practice of medicine, not to mention a new building. Later, he said that he was just in a foul mood. In the back of my mind something is telling me that he would never give up the practice of medicine, but he would give up being the business manager of the clinic. If that should happen, I would have to take his place or we would have to hire a business manager. My plan is to let it slide for a couple of weeks to see whether he becomes more attentive. If he doesn't, then it is time for a huge decision on my part. I have never questioned his business acumen, rather I have learned much watching how the business end is done. If Larry wants to make some personal changes then I think I am ready to take over in his stead.

The thought of being in charge of a project of that magnitude scares me to death. On the other hand, I have been at his side almost every step of the way and I think that, with his guidance, I could manage the site. I doubt that I would have to twist his arm if I offered to take the responsibility off his plate. I wonder how a construction crew would like to be questioned by a woman.

The child care program and center in the former garage behind the Clinic is ready to accept children. They will open the first of June. Julia has hired another woman to assist her and has also given Catherine and a couple of Catherine's friends, two hours of employment after school, three days a week. It's just the right amount of time for the girls to be working. I don't know whether the jobs will continue in September, but studies come first and I don't want any of them to get behind or have to give up any of their after-school activities because they are working. The position will be a great way to keep Catherine occupied during the summer months.

I am so glad that Julia has work to compensate for what I might not be paying her if I must make a temporary move to await the completion of the new house.

Julia and Larry, as you saw when you were here, are very much in love. It wouldn't surprise me at all if they decided to wed! A Catholic married to an Episcopal Deacon! There's one for the books!

That is all of my news at the moment, dear sister.

With love to all,
Margaret

May 10, 1949

Dearest Margaret,

Our four days together were "fantastic." I am not sure that I have ever written that word before but it certainly describes our Easter weekend. I too saw the girls as women for the first time. All three are indeed beautiful and intelligent. I was shocked each time they walked into the room. Catherine is so clever and has so many talents and such a sense of adventure. I cannot image what life will bring her but I can safely predict that she will never be bored. I recognize many of those same traits in Keiko. Maemi is the only one of the three that I can imagine settling happily in one place, at least while they are young.

What can I say of William and Bert? They are handsome, intelligent, brilliant, sweet and polite all at the same time. Thomas was amazed as well. Since our visit, he has talked much about them and about his and Charles' lives when they were about that same age. He pointed out that you and Charles married when you were but a year older than William. I was particularly affected by the relationship all five of our children seem to share. I suppose they will scatter to the four corners of the earth but I cannot imagine that they will not stay connected through letters, occasional get togethers and family events for the rest of their lives. Thomas was struck by how much William resembles Charles at the same age.

When he talks of the past, he remembers himself as being an integral part of your family and fondly describes celebrating holidays at your house. He now admits that, even though he enjoyed being part of your family, he never thought of marrying himself. You must have been in shock when you received the 1943 letter in which I reported our precipitous wedding. I myself am stunned at the memory of that weekend. However, at the time it seemed like the most natural thing in the world.

Speaking of love, I did sense that Larry and Julia have fallen. You have an uncanny ability to sense people who belong together and an extraordinary talent for seeing that they meet. Larry has been through so many changes since Karen passed away. I am happy that he is finding a sense of purpose in the church and a new chance for happiness. His changes open up possibilities for you as well.

It was exciting to see your three-dimensional house emerge from a two-dimensional plan and begin to take its place in time and space. How does it compare with your expectations? I truly do not know how you keep so many irons in the fire at one time but I certainly admire your ability.

Your future neighbors sound very interesting. I have a difficult time imagining someone who speaks in the present and past tense without transition. I sense his sister is aware that he is unusual. Why else would she keep trying to move the conversation to another subject? I look forward very much to hearing more about the Cottrells.

I assume that the business partner in your clinic will be one of the physicians. If you took such a position would you still be able to see patients? My mind boggles at the responsibility and yet I have not one iota of doubt that you will succeed in such a venture. You are an excellent organizer with an ability to deflect problems before others see them coming.

I do hope that Forey and Martin can be with us at the lake this summer. I am sorry to tell you that she is no longer expecting. Both she and Martin were devastated, particularly since there was no warning. They are grateful that they had not told her family. Forey and I talked together for hours. I hope that sharing my own experience of losing a child five years ago was helpful to her. They plan to wait a bit and consult a specialist before they make another attempt at starting a family.

Maemi and I drove to Pasco last Saturday. We enjoyed exploring the town. Unlike Richland, which was evacuated and recreated in 1942, Pasco has a history dating back to 1891 and several substantial two-story brick buildings line the main street. On the day of our visit, the town was abuzz with the news of a body that had been found in an alleyway earlier that same morning. I was all ears because I am still haunted by the disappearance of Emily Mayview's uncle-in-law, Gustav Schnaudlander (for whom her husband, Gus, was named).

He had boarded the train at the Ritzville station in a poor state of health, declaring that he would see the family homestead once more before he died. The few facts that I overheard about the body in the alley convinced me that it was not Uncle Gus. From what I have learned about security in the White Bluffs area, I believe that his determination to return to his old homestead ended his life.

When I meet with Emily and Gus next week, I will attempt to convey to them that he could not have reached his destination accidentally. The area is signed, barricaded, fenced and guarded. If he persisted, I believe that he intended it to be his last action. According to Emily, he had become very infirm and could no longer work. Work had been his life.

I am happy to report that Bustling Betty's Atomic Frontier Day tablecloth team has already created 40 table sets and has raised its goal to 100. Don't be surprised if you find one under your

Christmas tree. I must admit that Maemi and Keiko are doing most of my part of the work.

I thought that I had adapted well to being a traditional housewife but now realize that my brain was churning all the time. Now that it is challenged at work, I enjoy my time at home even more. In truth, there is little housework to do. The girls are perfectly willing and able to help. Thomas was a bachelor for quite some time and, therefore, does not require anyone to wait on him.

However, at least one of our neighbors has a husband who does want a servant wife. Last Tuesday my current next-door-neighbor, Gloria Smith, came over to visit and lost track of time. She suddenly jumped up all-of-a-tither, looked frightened and blurted out that she had to leave or she would not be ready when her husband got home. I asked her what she needed to do and she told me that when he came through the door he liked to see her in a nice dress wearing fresh makeup and holding out a drink to him. She seemed panicked because there was not enough time to arrange her hair in the style that he liked best, which took her an hour to achieve. Gracious heavens, dear Margaret— can you even imagine such a life? Words rarely fail me but they do now.

In my work I have been training others on new equipment. In my spare time, I read and research about international nuclear politics in my struggle to put my work into some sort of context. How does something that never before existed fit into the post-war world? Nearly all the information I need to carry my research forward is classified. I find myself nibbling at the edges and have discovered that the development of nuclear energy was known

by the English term "Tube Alloys" before the Americans renamed it the Manhattan Project.

**Please give my love to all,
Moira**

June 1, 1949

Dearest Moira,

I have so many snippets of news that I don't know where to begin! I'll just jump in and hope I can stay afloat!

Catherine loves the work she is doing under Julia's guidance at the child care center. The site has been named "Montrose Playhouse." The exterior really does look like a playhouse; the yard looks like the walled hiding place in *The Secret Garden.* I want to play there myself. Catherine has a very vivid imagination and loves reading to the children and then encourages them to act out the stories. Those private drama lessons have really paid off! She has the children dancing with scarves and making paper mâche puppets to use with the little stage she is helping Julia construct.

Julia and Larry have announced their engagement, though no date has been set and no mention of who will be performing the ceremony. It will be interesting to see how the Episcopal deacon-to-be and the devout Catholic will work out the arrangements.

The boys will be home in early August for a few days. I plan to be at the cottage the entire month; Catherine will be there as well. If you and Thomas can get the time off, perhaps you four will be able to spend time with us. If not, why not send the girls ahead and you two can come for whatever time you can spare?

The cabin of which I spoke is, indeed, available for the first two weeks in August...I hope that Forey and Martin will take one or both weeks. Please tell them of the availability and ask them to call the owners by Tuesday of next week (Temple-8-1659). David and Marcia Rogers will hold the cottage until then before offering it to someone else. I'm amazed that it was available, though Marcia said that they had had a cancellation!

I'm so sorry to learn of the Evans' loss and very glad that you were there to help Forey through this difficult time. Remember too, that Martin must be heart-broken. Like Larry struggling to find a cure for his wife, Martin could do nothing to save them the sorrow of losing their child. Perhaps Thomas could be of comfort? He well knows the pain of losing a child.

Larry has turned over the new clinic construction to me and we are hunting for a business manager for the practice. It would be ideal to find a candidate who has both a business and a medical background, but that may be just wishful thinking. I am feeling instant relief in not having to manage both the business and the construction.

Preparation of the ground is nearly complete. Because Spokane's South Hill is mainly basalt rock, parts of the clinic site have taken longer to excavate. In fact, we will only have a partial basement. We ran into too much rock, which made the cost to remove it sky-rocket. Barring any more unforeseen glitches, we should be pouring concrete by the end of the month.

Sarah and her husband Lloyd have returned to Spokane. Life in Israel was their choice and they loved their work. But when Sarah found she was pregnant, they decided that that unstable part of the world was not where they wanted to raise a family. The armistices between Israel and Jordan, Syria, Lebanon and Egypt are encouraging, but Palestinian "infiltrators" are being killed by Israeli Security Forces weekly. I can certainly understand their reasoning for not wanting to live under the constant threat of a possible incident. Lloyd is now looking for work. I doubt that it will be too difficult for him to find a position and Sarah may change her mind about working once the baby comes. For the time being, she is going to fill-in for our nurses while they are on vacation.

As for the Cottrells, I have discovered more oddities. Last week on one of my Manito Park walks, I came upon James mowing the grass of a home near mine. He was working with another man. Both were dressed as you would expect hired gardeners to be clothed. When I stopped and said, "Hello," he seemed nervous and perhaps a little embarrassed. The following day, I saw him again while I was at our new home site. He avoided me, though Marianne, his sister, did not. When I told her that I had seen James earlier in the week, she seemed very surprised! She said that he had been ill most of the week with a head-cold! I wonder whether he is telling her one thing and doing something else.

It seems so very childish, not to mention strange, to be sneaking out of the house to be a landscaper when he said that he was a University of Washington professor. I must solve this riddle. Somehow I'll have to confirm James' employment at the University; if I can think of a way to do so.

Larry has a week-long retreat scheduled which will take him out of town for several days. It is to be held in Seattle at St. Mark's. He plans to stay for a few extra days to visit with his daughter who lives in Edmonds and to attend the opening of the Seattle-Tacoma International Airport. Larry is somewhat of an airplane buff and is very interested to see the "state-of-the-art" terminal which cost over $3,000,000.00 to construct and the commercial airliners and military planes which will be on the tarmac for viewing the day of the dedication. Perhaps he can do some sleuthing into the Cottrells for me while he is there.

As for your neighbor, Gloria…what would happen if she were not at the door with cocktail in hand? It sounds to me that her husband is abusive. Watch for signs of bruising!

I am pleased that you are finding work satisfying; not to mention my envy in hearing that your girls are helping with the housework. I'm afraid that I have spoiled Catherine by having had Yoshi and Julia to manage the house. None of the children were asked to do much. They had weekly chores: weeding, mowing, the trash and keeping their rooms tidy. But other than the occasional time in the kitchen helping with Toll House Chocolate Chip cookie baking, none of them is really prepared for living on their own.

Am I correct in thinking that you are working with some sort of computer system like those you saw in New York and in Maryland? What do you mean when you say you spend time "researching" information that is classified? I hope that doesn't mean that you are places where you shouldn't be. It always worries me when you get overly curious. Do be careful! A library sounds much more secure and safe for doing research than skulking around the site.

I'm eager to learn of your summer plans and hope that you and the Evans will find a way to be with us at Newman Lake.

With love,
Margaret

June 15, 1949

Dearest Margaret,

As always, I was so happy to hear from you.

You may already know that Forey and Martin have booked the Rogers' cabin for the first two weeks in August. We are all thrilled. I know that being at the Lake will give them a chance to heal. Life since they married has been dramatic and busy and tragic but they seem to be doing well.

We will be there for as much of the month as possible. Atomic Frontier Days begin on August 11 this year and continue through the 14th so I imagine that we will need to be here in Richland for at least part of that time despite the fact that it will be very, very hot.

What ever could be going on with James? I find it very suspicious. Why would he take on multiple identities? For what reason would he masquerade as a professor *and* a gardener? His changing the tense of his verbs makes me even more curious. Could it be that English is not his native language? If he is consciously trying to maintain two identities he is certainly not meeting with much success. Of course, occasionally such behavior can be put down to eccentricity. I know that you will soon get to the bottom of this puzzle and eagerly await your discoveries.

I must say that I am relieved to hear that Sarah and Lloyd have returned from Israel. I do admire their dedication to creating a homeland. However, the area is very unsettled and nothing changes one's priorities more than having a child. I have no doubt that they will find another way to contribute to the state of Israel during their lifetimes and I cannot imagine that Lloyd will not find a position quickly.

How kind of you to create a place in your clinic where Sarah can work as a temporary employee.

Remember when pregnancy was called "confinement" and women hid themselves away during that time of life? There has been little change. Teachers still must resign their positions when they learn they are to have a child. This certainly didn't impact the school I attended in England. Every teacher there was a maiden lady.

At least here in Richland, working women are still looked down upon, nearly scorned. I was both amused and annoyed last week. I was sitting at home and reading with the front door open when Bella, a neighbor whose voice could shatter glass, strolled down the street while obviously giving a neighborhood orientation tour to a newcomer. First she described the family next door while pointing at their house. Next she gestured toward our house and said: "The family living there are the Walkers. *She* works." Those last two words were uttered with such disdain that they could have been "*She* has been accused of arson and murder."

It is strange that you mentioned Elizabeth Sterling Soule in an earlier letter. She was discussed in Keiko's class when they were studying a unit on local professional women. Keiko was very excited. Who knows, you may meet her in your new neighborhood if she visits her friend Marianne Cottrell.

Catherine is so creative and fun loving. I would love to see her work with the children and watch their faces beam in happiness as they dance and act out their stories at the Montrose Playhouse. What a perfect match for her talents! Likewise, your position in the clinic sounds just right for you. You certainly do not want to give up your work in medicine for that of construction management.

I am sure it will not surprise you to learn that Gloria Smith and her husband are now gone from our neighborhood. Two weeks ago, we heard screaming and banging at her house around midnight. Law enforcement vehicles roared onto the grass before we could lift the telephone to call for help. An ambulance followed and someone was immediately taken away on a gurney. The house was under repair by the time we woke up the next morning. Of course, nothing was said and before two weeks had passed, a new family was being welcomed into the neighborhood.

You asked some questions about my work. To tell you the truth until just a couple of days ago I had no clue what I was doing. Something Thomas said started me thinking and now I may perhaps understand my role.

Since my journey I have been spending time in a room with an enormous computing machine. Girls and women wearing sensible shoes constantly reprogram it by moving and readjusting and connecting wires, which is very tedious work.

I, however, do not connect wires. My duties are different nearly every day. The only predictable work is when guests are being ushered through the computer room. On those days, I adhere to a certain routine after changing into one of the three gabardine suits that hang in a special closet alongside appropriate blouses. When guests arrive on short notice, I quickly change into one of the outfits and assume a seat at a table in the corner of the area. On the table are piles of punch cards, a notebook and official looking papers, some in a leather folder and others in a tidy pile behind it.

My assignment is to appear to be busy while carefully watching the passing line of visitors who are accompanied by expert guides who work for the Atomic Energy Commission. Every single admiral, general, movie star, tycoon, and ordinary person is accompanied through the area. No one—absolutely no one—comes through unaccompanied; not even the head of the FBI, J. Edgar Hoover, himself.

My assignment is to write notes on general types of people, my impressions, etc. I have always loved watching people. During the first few tours that came through I felt more like I was a character in a play than a person doing real work. My role is to press a nearly invisible signal button if someone I recognize enters the room.

I have pressed the button only twice. Both triggered an identical response. Two men very quietly entered the room, one from the entrance door and one from the exit door. Before the doors closed, I slipped out through the exit door. All was accomplished with such subtlety that I doubt I would have noticed had I been one of the visitors. The first time was actually a rehearsal, though of course, I did not know that. A Hanford worker who attends our church walked through while wearing a disguise. In the second case, I recognized a person with whom I had talked at a dinner in London before the girls arrived.

I was puzzled but interested when one evening Thomas began to talk about the newly named condition known as prosopagnosia (Greek for "face not knowing"). The term describes someone who cannot recognize faces—not their mother's face, not their father's face, not even their own face. It is sometimes genetic and in other cases it is caused by an accident.

He asked what it would be like to be at the other end of the spectrum where one remembered every face they had ever seen. I thought it a strange question at the time. However, several days later I realized that I am a person who never forgets a face. In other words I am a "super recognizer." There is no unpronounceable word to describe those of us with that condition.

Perhaps it is strange to discover this at age 44. But, on the other hand, how would I know? I assume that others see things the same way that I do. And, of course, it is not strange to recognize every face one sees when one lives in a small village such as Brackham Wood.

It is going to take some time for me to adjust to this new knowledge. I am now beginning to see how the assignments I have been given lately fit together.

I can anticipate your next question: Is it dangerous to be in such a situation? I will think dear cousin; I will think.

I look forward to your next letter and to seeing you very soon.

Love,Moira

July 1, 1949

Dearest Moira,

I am definitely *not* going to give up patient care for the sake of construction management. However, I must admit to enjoying the learning process that goes along with the building of a new structure! I think my satisfaction is enhanced because both Larry and I have been able to breathe since we hired a clinic manager.

You may have already guessed who the individual is and if you thought Lloyd Jacobs, you are correct! Lloyd considered an ER position at Sacred Heart Hospital, but the hours he would be at work conflicted with Sarah's present and future schedule. After their experience in Israel, they have decided that they want to have as much family time together as possible. Their baby has yet to arrive, but when that day comes, Sarah will take time off from work at the Clinic to care for the child. Once old enough, the baby can be cared for at "Montrose Playhouse" should Sarah decide to return to work. It goes without saying that Lloyd's medical degree and business acumen places the clinic in good stead.

Larry is more involved than ever in his preparation for the diaconate and in the day to day work of St. John's. Construction of the Cathedral, which began in 1925, is expected to be completed by 1954. Interestingly, the cottage home made of stone and timber of the Cathedral's architect, Harold Whitehouse, is almost complete. The home is on Plateau Road about three blocks from the one that I am building.

One afternoon as I was taking a walk in the neighborhood, I saw Harold and his wife in the yard. He recognized me from a church committee upon which we both serve and invited me to come in for a cup of tea.

The varnished built-in cupboards and bookcases, windows, doors, entry tiles, and copper gutters look very much like that of the Cathedral itself, though not on such a grand size. Harold will use the detached garage not only for his car, but also for drafting and his hobbies of wood crafting and welding. Larry has asked him to create a myrtle wood crucifix for his Ordination. Harold showed me his first drafts for the piece. It will be beautiful.

I am sorry to hear about your friend, Gloria. I guess you have become hardened to the realities of what happens in cases like hers, but you must wonder who was on the gurney. The description of life with a husband who demands pearls, upswept hair, and a drink upon his arrival home sounds like an abusive one at best!

I am intrigued by the description of your work and I am familiar with the term "prosopagnosia," though I have never seen a patient with the condition. How your brain processes what you see when you look at a face is beyond amazing!

Perhaps you subconsciously look for birthmarks, scars, moles, freckles, wrinkles and the like. Plastic surgeons developed their skills during the past two wars and are now able to apply their techniques to patients having birth defects, and to those who have suffered injuries in automobile or industrial accidents. Aging of an individual would be problematic, but for plastic surgery. People with evil intent can change their features. How will that effect what you are able to do? I wonder what computers could do to assist in facial recognition!

Moira, you are finally in a place where after all the years of being under the direction of someone else, you can determine your own destiny. Your ability to do something that few can do, creates a niche for you. You will get your education on the job, but you will be able to take your ability "to market" so to speak and I would dare say be in demand by our government or law enforcement at the very least.

Then there is your capability to sort, categorize, and file. To me, it is as if you have the human equivalent of the abilities of one of computers with which you work. If you could somehow put your "super recognizer" skills together with your other assets, you would be able to contribute to the improvement of the computer's abilities. You may have just created a career for yourself! Congratulations!

However, despite all the heartfelt congratulations, I do wonder about the "special closet" ostensibly holding your work clothes. That scenario sounds like shades of your "watcher" days in Highgate. You have a variety of specialized talents that could make you the perfect spy! Seriously, what are you doing?

As for the continuing saga of James Cottrell...

In 1947, a year after Washington State Republican Albert Canwell came into the Legislature, he introduced a "resolution to create a committee with broad powers to investigate organizations whose membership included Communists." One of those organizations to be investigated was the University of Washington.

Canwell was elected as the Chairman of the Joint Legislative Fact Finding Committee on Un-American Activities. Hoping to eradicate the Communist Party, the Committee held public hearings, the agenda of which was to expose the Party members. The hearings however, were one-sided. The accused could not cross-examine their accusers, nor could they make any statements. Many of the accused were not active members, or had left the Party years before. Some were not even Communists. But the accusations cost many their reputations as well as their jobs. James Cottrell falls into the category of "having once was, but no longer is," a Communist. He left his position at the University rather than go through investigations. I do not think that his tense discrepancies have anything to do with attempting to cover the fact that he is not an American. I pose that he may have suffered a break and has determined that he must be rid of all connections to his former life. Marianne may not agree with him and so he is lying to her as well as anyone new to him.

This information came to me through "a friend of a friend," of David Stewart who lived in the same neighborhood as James Cottrell and knew David through work at Boeing. I'm still amazed in what a small world we coexist; I asked Gillian whether she had ever heard of James and within days David was calling me with the story. I don't know where to go with my relationship with my neighbors. Do you have any thoughts?

I'm so looking forward to our time at the Lake and so happy that Forey and Martin will be there as well. I hope not to stick out like a sore thumb as the unattached female! I can't believe that I am worrying about that! The reality of being alone in a couple of years is finally hitting home!

With love to all,
Margaret

July 12, 1949

Dear, Dear Margaret,
   We all look forward to seeing you in a few days. Maemi and Keiko have so much to tell Catherine that she may not get a word in. We are all anxious see William and Bert. I think that all five of them will all have much more in common than ever before. Even though she is the youngest, or perhaps because of it, Keiko is a very mature 13-year-old.

   I am relieved that you no longer need to worry about clinic management. Lloyd Jacobs is a very good fit for the position. I sense that you had a great deal to do with his placement.

I write this letter from my basement. Do you remember me asking neighbors why they had furniture in their cellar and their reply: "You will understand this summer." They were correct. It is hot here, very hot. Hotter than I could have imagined. My comfortable chair and small table serve me well. My bare feet rest comfortably on a braided rag rug and I am relaxed.

I must admit, however, that the unrelenting sun and long hours of daylight can become oppressive. The average daily high temperature this month has reached 92 degrees. Bright sun bleaches the landscape and I wear sunglasses whenever I go out of doors. We all manage to find ways to cool off. The following example will give you nightmares as a medical professional. Every month, when the Benton County Mosquito Abatement District truck comes through the city, a crowd of children joyfully ride their tricycles and bicycles in the wonderful cool clouds of DDT that spray from its back. They joke that DDT means "Drop Dead Twice."

But then children always find ways to have fun even when it puts them in harm's way. On the two days that snow covered the ground last winter, these same children go "hooky bobbing" which means that they grab onto the back fenders of moving cars and skid along behind.

My work is extremely varied at this time. I honestly do not know where I will be, what I will be doing, or what I will wear until I reach the part of the plant where I have been assigned for that day. Occasionally I resume my seat at the desk in the computer area and "sort cards" while individuals are escorted past the computer. Happily, the room is kept cool, which is no small feat given the fact that it contains nearly 17,500 vacuum tubes plus resistors and capacitors. All this is held together by millions of hand-soldered joints. In contrast, the Philco radio in our home runs on only five tubes.

Each day I report to my assigned area where I am given a short briefing and, if necessary, a description of any required wardrobe changes. I have a number of outfits at my disposal. Some of them are slimming and some add 30 pounds to my frame. For example, one day I may wear a bandana, coveralls, sensible shoes and carry a tool kit. The following day I am dressed in a white uniform serving food in the cafeteria. I rarely spend more than four hours in one of these costumes. One day my immediate supervisor did not recognize me. When I told him who I was he broke out in hearty laughter and said that I was doing a great job.

I was pleased to hear that my job description has virtually nothing to do with my daily duties at the plant. Occasionally, I feel concern that someone may become aware of my recognition skills. Perhaps I am put into these costumes for my own protection. I amuse myself by playing a mental game of *Clue*. One day I am "the window cleaner up a ladder with a squeegee" and the next I am "the secretary in the office with a shorthand pad."

I am amused but not surprised at how quickly you were able to discover the truth about James Cottrell. You would make an excellent detective. I am surprised, however, that his sister does not know his story. Perhaps she knows but does not tell. However, I am deeply distressed by Senator Albert Canwell's use of fear and intimidation. One-sided hearings during which the accused are unable to cross-examine their accusers or make their own statements and many are losing their jobs because of a former party alliance sounds more like Nazi Germany than America.

I hear a slight echo of the students at Cambridge University before the beginning of the last war. The Fascists and the Communists were at loggerheads. All were idealistic and brilliant students. However, they adhered to diametrically opposed ideals. Those who leaned toward Fascism wanted to appease Germany and prevent the war. The students who joined the Communist party preached the gospel of equality for all, which appealed to those who saw the lower classes living on the edge of starvation while the privileged upper classes lived in consummate luxury. I find this ironic since many of the Communist students were children of privilege and living very well at college.

Perhaps they found Communism a romantic notion in the 1930s. They did not recognize that life in the Soviet Union was not as good as they imagined. Despite being born of wealth they were needy and not well parented.

Now, both Americans and British are very concerned about the growing hostilities with the Soviet Union. The countries were not easy bedfellows during the war and things have worsened since. Last year when the USSR blockaded the path to partitioned Berlin, many feared the imminent onset of World War III. Berlin then became a symbol of the United States' resolve to stand up to the Soviet threat without being forced into a direct conflict. The Berlin Airlift prevented the USSR from isolating the city. They lifted the blockade earlier this summer. There are still checkpoints and searches but Berlin is once again accessible.

I think that our nuclear superiority gives us the confidence to stand up to forces of Stalin. The security provisions at all sites in the Manhattan Project have been, and continue to be, extremely tight. General Groves allowed each employee to know only as much as he needed to know to complete the task immediately before him.

But enough of this. In a few days we will be enjoying our time together at the lake and thoughts of WWIII will be far from our minds.

I must warn you that Forey thinks that I am losing some of my British expressions and picking up Americanisms. Apparently I now use the American pronunciation of "garage."

Much love until then,
Moira

September 6, 1949

Dearest Moira,

I cannot believe that summer is over and our "children" have gone back to school! The days of summer, especially the month of August, have given me so many wonderful memories that I find myself happy at the very thought of them.

Catherine will take the SAT next month. She doesn't seem to be in the least way concerned, so I do not remind her of the importance of doing well. I hear from Julia that she and her friends talk about the test incessantly while working at the "Playhouse." Julia says that the girls have formed a Math Study Group...on their own....so I know Catherine is concerned and will do her very best!

However, having just bragged excessively about her, I must tell you that Catherine can also be a terror! Last weekend, she and her friend, Sheila, decided to pool their money and buy tickets for a train-ride to Seattle. Sheila's brother attends the University of Washington and had promised them tickets to see the UW/Notre Dame Football match. They caught the midnight train and were in Seattle by 8 a.m. in plenty of time to see the game. They were back on the train and home early Sunday morning. All the while I thought that the girls were with Sheila's family for the weekend and Sheila's family thought their daughter was with us! The rest of the story is not pleasant, so I will only say that both girls are grounded for a very long while. They can use their punishment time studying for the Scholastic Aptitude Tests! Also unpleasant was the final score of the game in which Notre Dame bested UW 27-7.

A young Spokane mother, a patient in our clinic, died recently from the polio virus. She had given birth just before the disease was diagnosed and had spent most of the last days of her life in an iron lung. The disease seems to be on the increase as witnessed by the 300+ cases this year in our state alone, 63 of them are in Spokane County. In spite of the research, the medical community just can't prevent the dreaded disease. Bert continues to do polio research work with Dr. Paffenbarger when he is not in class. I pray that the good doctor, who also works with Dr. Jonas Salk, can come up with a vaccine soon!

I'm so grateful that Bert has little disability as a result from his bout with polio. He was so fortunate. On the other hand, the number of cases in the County frightens the population. Most people believe the disease is attributed to unsanitary conditions, and yet patients who have been struck down were not living unhygienically, which makes them even more afraid that they too will be infected.

Julia recently told me that the child care center had purchased *Candy Land*, a game invented by a woman, who herself was recuperating from polio, in a clinic in San Diego. Julia says the children who can't read or count yet love the new game as they progress around the game board by taking turns removing the top card from a stack, most of which show one of six colors, and then moving their marker ahead to the next space of that color.

The Chronicle reported that last April, a group of businessmen who are interested in promoting athletics in Spokane met and within six hours, had plans for what has since been named Memorial Stadium. They had no money to pay for it, but nonetheless hired a contractor, agreed on the price, and have gone out into the community to other like-minded business men to get the needed funding. The committee is made up of men from all the private clubs in the city. Everyone agrees that a stadium is something that all citizens would enjoy and support. It will have a seating capacity of 25,000 and is to be located on the former site of Baxter Army Hospital where I worked during the war. The grass field will be taken from sod from the parade grounds at Fort George Wright. Finally high schoolers will have a great field upon which to play their Merry-Go-Round tournament! It is thought that the structure can be built in less than six months. That is amazing!

Does it really bother Forey that you have lost some of your British expressions? I didn't want to bring up the question while we were together. Perhaps it's a good thing to have Americanized your speech. I was quite amazed at the sound of your tongue. You could have fooled even me into thinking that you had been born and raised in the United States. Perhaps you have another talent...fooling someone into thinking that you are anything but British! While at the Lake, you seemed to slip back into the vernacular only when you were totally relaxed; otherwise I would have thought you had lost your "Britishness" too. Perhaps you subconsciously want to sound American?

As for your job...it sounds to me that you are working much more than you had ever planned. It is as if every day you are playing "Charades," except not for fun. I doubt that anyone will discover your ability to "recognize," but I suppose that the skill could be noted in your employee records and anyone with access to those, could learn of your aptitude. Are you able to see your records? Can Thomas check to learn whether your "talent" is noted on file? Now I have another reason to worry about you!

Indeed, our nuclear capability gives us some degree of security. However, I worry about the Communist threat and what it will do to our country when so many are accused of being Communist but aren't. The accusations alone can ruin lives. The other side of the coin is that the real Communists can go on undetected, "sleeping" so to speak, and poised to do real damage.

Communists... I haven't seen either of the Cottrells in a very long time. Their curtains are drawn and the lawn appears to be very dry. When I think about it, I haven't seen them since I left for the Lake in early August. I wonder where they could be?

Then there is the unrest along the 38th parallel. Surely that doesn't mean that the United States will again be involved in a war in Korea!

I hate to close on such a depressing thought, so I won't. I want you all to know what sheer joy it was to be with you and how much Catherine and the boys loved being together as well. We have so much for which to be thankful.

With love,
Margaret

September 15, 1949

My Dear Margaret,

It was nearly impossible for us to wrench ourselves away from the cabin last month. Forey and Martin think the place is marvelous and have become passionate about buying a cabin there. They would much prefer one that is already standing, even if in a primitive state. Failing that, they want to buy property. They are both terribly busy right now so I promised I would mention this to you in my next letter, in the event that you hear of an available property. Neither of them has ever dreamed of owning such a place of escape. We are amused that in France a second home is called a *pied-à-terre* while in England it is called a "bolt hole."

Catherine! Oh my, what a shock! I have full confidence in her ability to plan, travel and have fun. However, this is a terrible way to demonstrate such talents. I have heard it said that girls are sneakier than boys, who will loudly declare they are leaving, slam the door and face the consequences later. I am glad that you have imposed consequences that she will not soon forget. I have learned from listening to neighbors that imposing a consequence is one thing, monitoring it and making sure it is fulfilled is another. As a mother of two girls, not much younger than Catherine, I have been thinking about this a lot.

I have serious questions about Sheila. You no doubt know her parents but I wonder about her strong powers of persuasion. Knowing Catherine as

I do, I cannot imagine her trying such shenanigans. I wonder why she felt she had to lie. Did she think you would say no? Did she think what she was doing was wrong? Did she just want to experience the excitement of escaping? However my major question is whatever made her think she could outsmart the smartest of mothers.

We have seen many cases of polio here. A vaccine that can prevent it will be such a relief. People who fear any disease want to believe that it is impossible for them to be affected. The myth that polio thrives only in unsanitary conditions gives them that feeling of control. They believe that if they merely keep their surroundings clean they will not be affected. Just imagine our Bert having a part, no matter how small, in the development of a vaccine that would prevent this terrible disease and put our minds at rest.

How exciting to imagine a stadium on the site of Baxter Hospital! I suppose it will be used for events that we cannot even imagine. What fun it will be for you to cheer for your favorite team in the same place on the earth where you once worked.

The wonderful time we spent at the Lake with you all followed by our return home for Atomic Frontier Days strengthened our resolve to return to the Spokane area. We have decided that, when the time is right, we will be willing to sacrifice a great deal to return. Luckily, we still own our home there and I am sure that Thomas will be able to find work. With two girls approaching college age we feel that we need to be responsible and not make a wild move but, on the other hand, there are opportunities for higher education in Spokane and nearby.

William's enthusiasm for television whet his uncle's appetite for that field. Of course, he has no experience in that area but then very few people do. However, he certainly has experience in journalism. It may be some time before Spokane gets a station, however. Immediately after the war ended, the Federal Communications Commission was flooded with applications for TV station licenses. Last year, unable to keep up with the demand, they ordered a freeze on processing any additional applications. Trapped in the stoppage was Bing Crosby's application for stations in Spokane, Tacoma, and Yakima. Right now no one knows how long until the freeze thaws but hopes are high that it will happen soon.

I am very concerned about the Cottrell brother and sister. Would it be possible for you to call some type of social services to check on their welfare? If their bills are paid and they have few friends it is possible that they could have come to harm in their own home. These witch hunts for Communists are very disturbing. I imagine that people are afraid to stand up for their friends for fear they themselves will be targeted.

I very much appreciate your concern about my safety and I do not discount it. I shall give it serious thought. Obviously, I understand why it would be valuable to have an employee who can remember faces. Perhaps that is why I wear different outfits in my work. You will forgive me a little joke about a serious matter—perhaps I am a human Minox. I imagine records are kept on me because I am called in to a variety of situations but whether or not they are written and where they might be held is a complete mystery. This secret keeping business in both Britain and America is really quite interesting.

The Federal Bureau of Investigation (FBI) in the United States and the Directorate of Military

Intelligence, Section 5 (MI5) in Britain are both visible and public. For example the FBI agents who we see in Richland are highly identifiable with their slacks and shirts and high level of physical fitness. They live openly amongst us in the community. In London, members of MI5 can be easily identified by their bowler hats, umbrellas and presence on the street corners.

On the other hand, those who work for the CIA and Secret Intelligence service (MI6) strive to remain invisible. They might be your next door neighbor, or work in your bank. In fact, sometimes I wonder if Robert Gentry, the Englishman on whom I had my first crush, was not a member of MI6. He lived just across the street from me and was away for weeks at a time.

What is more frightening, however, is yesterday's announcement by President Truman revealing that on the 29th of last month the Russians successfully detonated a plutonium bomb identical to the one that fell on Nagasaki. If we are plunged into WWIII it will be a different animal. The last two were bad enough but the possibility that hundreds of thousands of people can be killed by one bomb is unfathomable.

In order for the Russians to have created a bomb this quickly it is obvious that they were closely following our progress here in the United States. This comes as a great shock to those of us who live amidst strong security precautions. We now realize that the Russians have been receiving detailed and specific information during every step in the development of nuclear weapons. In other words, the secrets, which we have all labored so hard to keep, have gone directly to the Russians.

Hanford workers have endured security checks day after day to reach their specific worksite; some of them passing through five checkpoints to weld a seam or pour cement. Children do not know what their fathers do at work. Wives never ask about their husband's day and are told to move to another room if he should talk in his sleep. All this secrecy seems to have been for naught.

We wish Catherine all the luck in the world with her SAT examination. How clever of her and her friends to form a Math Study Group! They obviously do not want their parents to know that they are secretly preparing for their examinations. I am sure that makes it much more fun. I wonder what sort of trouble you and I would have stirred up had we been together at that age.

With much love and appreciation,
Moira

October 4, 1949

Dearest Moira,

You cannot imagine how happy I am to hear you say that you have even *thought* of returning to Spokane! Your life in Richland has always sounded so full and interesting. I thought that I would hear you say that you were settled and never leaving there. You certainly won't find the same amount of excitement here! I doubt that any of my friends would ever consider that they might have an FBI or CIA agent living next door!

I know that Thomas would have no difficulty in finding work here; a position at the newspaper is probably his for the asking. KHQ-TV, a subsidiary of Cowles Publishing would be another possibility for a man with Thomas' credentials. Cowles is poised to go on the air as soon as they get the station license. All Thomas would need to do is walk in the front door of either the station or the newspaper and a job would fall in his lap. I didn't realize that the freeze on licensure might take so long! Bing Crosby competing with the Cowles for the first license! That will be interesting to watch!

I totally understand the need to be in a community where your girls have more support in their education. Most likely, the teachers at Columbia High School are as dedicated as the teachers are here. However, one wonders whether the Richland schools have the supplies, books and equipment that are found in a larger school district. Here, there are also private schools that can offer another option for your girls. The fact that there are two schools of higher education in Spokane also benefits high schoolers.

This may change your mind about moving back, however!

An eight year old girl disappeared from the North Side two weeks ago. The news has had front-page coverage for days. She had been selling candy for a school project with two other girls. She just disappeared from the front of the store where she and the others had been. The two other children had gone into the store momentarily and when they returned they found little Carol Richards gone. Today they found her body in a field west of town. She had been brutally strangled. It is unbelievable what her disappearance, and now her death, has done to the city's sense of security. I have never locked my doors; no one does. Now it is as if our city is in mourning for both the child and what has happened to our heretofore feeling of safety.

Dear Catherine! Thus far she has been very cooperative in following the restrictions which have been placed upon her. Receiving letters from both brothers regarding her behavior has also helped. I tend to agree with your assessment of Sheila. She is the youngest of six children and I think has been forgotten. Her parents are well respected, educated people but they are also very socially connected and spend a great deal of time climbing the ladder so to speak. Sheila, who is very bright, saw an opportunity and took it! As for Catherine, I believe she thought that she wouldn't get caught. I was involved with the election of the new Medical Society Officers that weekend and dropped the ball. I should have checked with Catherine after school before she left home to go to Sheila's to "spend the night." That is my routine whenever I am not going to be home until later in the evening.

If you and I had had the freedom that Catherine and her friends have had we might have had tea with the King! But alas, we did not have money to spend and trains to catch without someone in our village reporting us before we could even step onto the platform! Nonetheless, I would love to have had the opportunity to "stir up some trouble"… without getting caught, of course. That in itself sounds like Catherine. Perhaps there is little wonder why she pulled this escapade!

Please tell the Evanses that I will keep my ear to the ground regarding anyone who wishes to sell their property at Newman Lake. I will call Ben Silver, our caretaker, and make some further inquires.

I have, as you suggested, attempted to find out something; anything, about the mysterious disappearance of the Cottrells. It's been at least three months since last I saw either of them. F. S. Barrett Realty has put up a "For Sale" sign in their yard. Before that, a group of workmen removed all the furnishings from the house, or so say other neighbors. Today a realtor was at the property when I stopped by to check on my house. I asked him if he knew where the Cottrells had moved. He said he had never heard of the Cottrells and that the home was owned by the "Smith Trust." Marianne and James' disappearance is beginning to sound like a Hanford ejection of wayward employees!

Are you saying that there was an actual spy infiltrating the Manhattan Project? I suppose that is a silly question; but how else could the Russians get information on how to build such a bomb? If there was a spy living in Richland and going to work on the Reservation, where is that person now? Truman's announcement also begs the question, "Where did the Russians detonate it and what about the people living in the vicinity of the explosion?" The world is very much aware of what the "bomb" did to Nagasaki! What does it mean for the world to have two countries with nuclear capabilities?

Truman's revelation must have had some effect on your position and on your observations. Of one thing I am certain: you and Thomas have had multiple discussions about secrecy and lack thereof. I am relatively sure that the Russians are not the only country in the world with spies embedded in highly sensitive workplaces.

Moira, to me, this means that your work could be even more dangerous. Perhaps you have actually seen the spy and can identify him (I suppose it could be a her). It could mean that the spy knows who *you* are! Please get out of that place; sooner, rather than later. It is not safe for you, for Thomas, or for the girls. Your job was supposed to be working with computers, not bombs! No one knows what a desperate person would do if he/she were trying to get out of the country to avoid detection. I know you want to do your job well and see it to completion and I know you want to catch this person before he can get away, but please let the FBI or the CIA do the heavy lifting!

With love and concern for all of you,
Margaret

November 2, 1949

My Dear Margaret,

How good to hear from you! I am relieved to hear that Catherine is back to her old self. Asking her brothers to weigh in was a brilliant strategy. I am so grateful that all of our children are close. They will be able to rely upon one another when times become difficult.

We do look forward to living near you in Spokane once again. I think that the girls will make the transfer back into their old school district with very little trouble. They have had excellent teachers here, probably due to the federal monies that allowed the school district to offer some of the highest salaries in the state. Other federal monies that have been funneled into the Richland School District have allowed the purchase of extra supplies and equipment.

The story of Carol Richards is horrifying. Can you imagine losing a family member in such a tragedy? I am happy that our children are as old as they are. You and I have had good lives but have still learned that life sends us some unexpected challenges.

It sounds like Marianne and James never existed. How can this be? I wonder if they witnessed something or testified against a dangerous person.

Or perhaps they were on the run. Strange things seem to be happening everywhere.

You ask important questions about the Russian bomb. We are only just beginning to come to terms with the fact that Russia obviously had access to our scientific developments in this area. Our confidence in our nuclear superiority was shattered with one blow. We do need to discover how the Russians were able to gain access to this secure information.

I wish I could tell you how soon we will be in Spokane. It cannot be long now. We have not yet told the girls. They have friends here but I do not suspect that they will mind going home at all. They have been away from the Spokane schools only 19 months. They tell me that when they visit Spokane and spend time with Catherine and their old friends it seems as though no time has passed.

However, I predict that once they are established in their old routines, they will realize how they have changed and grown in the past year and a half. Their time in England gave them once-in-a-lifetime experiences, including going to an exclusive school for girls where they began each day in the chapel, wore uniforms and played new games. They also learned to operate in a new and confusing non-decimal monetary system and saw the tragic results of a world war. In addition, they were treated as celebrities when we spent a long weekend in Brackham Wood. They were even told that they sounded like movie stars.

One day they will appreciate those experiences but the only one they talk about constantly, in fact I am sure that they mention it every day, is having been houseguests in Forey's ancestral home and attending her wedding. They give reports, tell stories and show their pictures at every opportunity.

When they arrived at Richland they were instantly welcomed and became old timers in a matter of weeks. They were giving tours and welcoming and helping new students become adjusted within the month. I must believe that this time of disruption and adventure will serve them well for the rest of their lives.

I believed that the work that Thomas and I did in England and here in Richland was very important to the futures of both England and America. However, I must admit that recent worldwide developments have led me to question this optimistic evaluation.

I wish I could tell you when we shall arrive. I am so glad that you have offered to give us some assistance. It is a real benefit that we have continued to use the HEW furniture that Thomas bought from the former occupants of this house and left our own furniture in Spokane. Some is stored and other pieces are being used by our renters. All we will need to do is to pack up our personal belongings, which will make the move much easier.

You do know how much I appreciate you and am looking forward to living close to you again. However, Thomas and the girls may arrive in Spokane a bit before I do.

With much love and gratitude,

Your cousin and sister,
Moira

November 21, 1949

Dearest Moira,

Last month I was thrilled at the prospect of seeing *all* of you very soon. Now you tell me it may be Thomas and the girls arriving *before* you do. What on earth do you mean? What reason could keep you from returning at the same time as your family? Surely it is not your job! Or could it be? If it is does pertain to your job, I certainly hope that you are not playing some role in discovering what part the Russians played in the security breach!

I have expressed my fears for your safety numerous times and to put it bluntly, I have always thought that it was Thomas who was in constant danger. Now it seems that he is willing to blithely leave his position and *you* behind. He knows very well what could happen to you when you are alone. Why would he be party to a repetition of the London fiasco?

Please *both of you, listen to me!* Consider sending the children and your goods ahead and staying together for the completion of whatever it is that only Moira can accomplish!

My home on Scott Street is moving ahead of schedule; in fact, I am told that I will be able to take occupancy *before* Christmas! I will gladly care for the girls if it means that you and Thomas stay together to the end of whatever your mission is.

There is nothing more to tell about the Cottrells. The neighbors know nothing.

I am posting this letter as soon as I sign it. I have nothing more to tell you at this point other than to beg you to accept my offer to take care of the girls until you *both* can get here.

With love and reluctant trust in whatever you choose to do,
Margaret

*****

This last letter, written many years ago, put an abrupt end to the correspondence between the two cousins. Every time I reread it I am shocked by its tone. Margaret pleads with Moira to come to Spokane with the family and, if Moira must stay in Richland, she does not want her to stay alone.

Since it was included with the others, I assume that Mother read it before she left on this assignment. I have myself read it dozens of times and am stunned each and every time I do so. I am not shocked that Aunt Margaret advised my mother to come directly to Spokane with the rest of us or to send us ahead and come later with our father. However, I am shocked by Aunt Margaret's fear. I saw her frightened very few times in the years that I knew her and I recognize her fear in the directive tone of that letter.

Whenever she was faced with danger, Aunt Margaret displayed an extraordinary talent for seeing clearly what needed to be done and gave orders that no one would dare refuse. For example, shortly after Keiko and I joined the family, a fire broke out in a nearby house. Aunt Margaret took charge immediately. We were each ordered to pull the pillow out of our pillowcase and stuff it with our school supplies, travel kits and two days' clothing. In addition, we were each assigned one household item to carry. I was proud to be put in charge of the small steel suitcase that held the important family papers. I think we were all packed up and assembled by the kitchen door in ten minutes.

The fire down the street was extinguished quickly and, therefore, we did not need to carry out the rest of the plans. However, instead of sending us directly to bed, Aunt Margaret created a pleasant memory for us by stirring up a huge vat of hot cocoa and opening a box of graham crackers. The next morning we all regaled our classmates with the exciting night we had just spent. We five Walker offspring still reminisce about this incident when we get together.

Mother's complete disregard of her cousin's warnings bothers us to this day. We knew her as a person of moderation who was neither too bold nor too wary. However, there was an uncharacteristic urgency in this departure. After a brief goodbye, Mother merely walked out the door.

Mother left us and Richland in the early morning hours of November 27, 1949, the Sunday after Thanksgiving. One week later, Margaret opened her door to find Father, Keiko and me standing on her doorstep. Her face turned deathly white. Obviously, our father had not had the courage beforehand to tell Margaret that Mother had gone and that we would be coming as a threesome. I am sure that moment was agonizing for them both.

Catherine heard our voices and came running. We three girls then disappeared up the stairs to catch up on all our news and began arranging things for our stay. Looking back now, I wish I could have recorded the exchange that must have gone on between Aunt Margaret and her brother-in-law during those first hours. I would not have liked to have been in his shoes. By the time we were called down to dinner, lists of tasks had been drawn up and we were made to feel welcome and comfortable.

Keiko, Father and I had disappeared from our Richland house as quickly as the neighbors that Mother wrote about in her letters. Looking back from an adult perspective, I realize that Aunt Margaret was greatly disturbed during the weeks that passed until Mother returned safely. Perhaps it is good that she was also immersed in her career and preoccupied with the construction of a new clinic building as well as in the myriad of details involved in seeing her new house to completion. I remember that our father helped her a great deal during that time, which no doubt distracted him from his other concerns.

Mother returned to us five long weeks later. She was completely exhausted but, unlike her first arrival in Spokane, she rebounded quickly. Aunt Margaret moved into her new home when it was completed in December and we remained as her renters until the following summer when the lease ran out on our family home. With great joy, we took repossession of the home we had left two years prior. Aunt Margaret's 14th Avenue house sold almost immediately.

I am rather ashamed to say that, as a child, except for being away from Mother at Christmas, which was terrible, I remember this move back to Spokane as a fun and exciting time. Not only were we back with Catherine, but we reunited quickly with our old school and neighborhood friends who were fascinated by our tales of the adventures that we had experienced during the two years that we had been away.

I admit that I enjoyed overhearing some of the comments being made behind my back, such as: "She has been to England and Chicago and New York and has flown in an airplane and lived in another city besides Spokane. My life here is so boring".

A year-and-a-half after Mother's return, when Keiko, Catherine and I were totally involved in our high school activities, an item of international news hit our family like a ton of bricks. The newspaper headlines screamed the message that two British spies, Guy Burgess and Donald Maclean, who had both been heavily involved in English and American intelligence and counterintelligence, had disappeared from London and were suspected to have defected to Russia on May 25, 1951. These suspicions were soon confirmed.

Over the years since then, William has used his journalistic skills and instincts to almost certainly connect our mother with the activities of one of these two defectors.

Donald Maclean had first come to the United States in June of 1944, achieved the position of First Secretary to the British Ambassador and, toward the end of that period, served as Secretary of the Combined Policy Committee on atomic energy matters, a position that allowed him access to all information on the development of atomic weapons in the United States, Britain and Canada.

As time passed, we learned that Maclean had been recruited by the Communist Party while a student at Cambridge University and was later persuaded to become a Soviet Agent by his friend, Kim Philby. A son of the British upper class, Maclean was able to join the foreign office in 1937 at the young age of 24. As the British representative on the American-British-Canadian Council on the sharing of atomic secrets, he was able to provide the Soviet Union with the information from the Council meetings.

While he could not pass technical data on the atom bomb itself, he was able to share information on its development, particularly the amount of plutonium in the possession of the United States. That knowledge allowed Soviet scientists to accurately predict how many bombs could be built. Maclean was also privy to information on civil aviation, bases, and post-hostilities planning, which was also helpful to the Soviet Union.

William discovered that J. Edgar Hoover, head of the FBI, had been irritated to learn that Maclean was one of the few dignitaries allowed to visit nuclear plants unaccompanied, a privilege which Hoover himself was denied. With Maclean's defection, security officials in the United States realized that he had been freely sharing America's atomic secrets with Joseph Stalin.

Toward the end of his tenure in Washington D.C., Maclean's demeanor was affected by alcohol. He began talking too much as well as exhibiting drunken and wild behavior. He was then transferred to the position of head of Chancery at the British Embassy in Cairo. This Cairo connection grabbed our family's attention.

William and Bert both phoned immediately after this news broke. We had always suspected that the scarabs that Mother had brought back for each of us signified much more that their symbolic meaning of rebirth. They were also a clue as to where she had been. As more information about the defection of Maclean was revealed, we began to realize that she must have been involved in counter-espionage at the highest level.

We concluded that Mother had been sent to Egypt to use her skills as an invisible observer and super recognizer. Was she in Cairo to confirm Donald Maclean's behavior? Had she seen him in Whitehall during WWII? Could she identify him from pictures or from film? Had she learned about him on her forays to Cambridge? Was he perhaps one of the men visiting Karl Marx' grave in Highgate Cemetery? We still discuss these topics.

The next big revelation came twelve years later in January of 1963 when a third agent defected to Russia. Kim Philby, the man in charge of protecting the secrets of both the United States and Britain, had been an agent of the Soviet Union. He had not only been the head of British counter intelligence at MI6 but was also liaison to the American CIA, a position that had given him access to all secrets of both countries. It was he who had discovered that Maclean was about to be identified and in turn informed Soviet officials who then arranged for the defection of Maclean and fellow spy, Burgess, to Russia before either of them could be arrested and questioned. They knew too much.

Maclean, Burgess and Philby eventually became known as the first three members of the infamous Cambridge Five Spy Ring. The fourth and fifth spies did not defect and were not unveiled until years later. The fourth man, Sir Anthony Blunt, who was related to English royalty by virtue of being a third cousin to the Queen Mother, worked as the curator of the Queen's picture gallery in Buckingham Palace. The fifth was John Cairncross, who, while working at Bletchley Park during WWII, passed information on the enigma machine to Russia and also gave data on Britain's efforts to create an atomic bomb.

Blunt's Communist Party connection was hushed up quite effectively until Margaret Thatcher became Prime Minister of Great Britain. She saw to it that he was stripped of his knighthood in 1979. John Cairncross lived in the United States for a time and lectured at both Case Western and Northwestern Universities. At age 82, he returned to Britain, married his second wife, a 40-year-old American opera singer, and died one month later.

We suspect that Mother's assignments in Cambridge had something to do with gathering background on these five men and perhaps others as well.

However, in 1995, the release of the secret of the VENONA intercepts caused us to completely reevaluate the work my parents were doing during the Cold War. We have found indications that they, particularly my mother, were involved in what could possibly be the most dramatic counter-intelligence operation yet revealed.

These secret intercepts consisted of nearly 3,000 decrypted cables sent from Soviet agents in the United States to Russia between 1942 and 1946. While the existence of the VENONA decryption remained a secret, information from these decryptions had been circulated among American military and civilian security officials and to Congress. They, in turn, passed it on to journalists and commentators who released it to the general public. These revelations resulted in the identification of at least three members of the Cambridge Five spy ring in England and a massive investigation of members of the American Communist Party, which led to the 1953 execution of nuclear spies Julius and Ethyl Rosenberg.

The official release of the secret that these messages had been decoded, as well as the information in the first released messages, helped us understand why my parents suddenly relocated to London in 1947 and why they were transferred from there to Richland, Washington. The first message that was translated revealed that the Soviets had infiltrated America's most secret enterprise, the atomic bomb project. These cables had been written in what was thought to be an unbreakable code. In addition, cover names were substituted for those of the Soviet agents and their projects.

The code was truly unbreakable by design. However, some of the one-time-pads used for encryption were reused, allowing a small percentage of the messages sent from Soviet agents in the US to the USSR to be decoded.

The decryption of one of the cables revealed that a physicist, code-named MAR, who had been hired at Hanford in October of 1943, was a Soviet agent. Could he have been the Marvin that Mother was expecting to meet with on her first day of work at Hanford; the

Marvin that she mentioned in her letter of March 13, 1949? If that was the case, it perhaps can explain our move to Richland and our parents' involvement there.

Even today, the Hanford Reservation continues to be a mystery. Evidence points to radiation exposure affecting many living in its shadow and located downwind from the site. But not all the secrets of Hanford's bi-products have been released to the general public. My Aunt Margaret saw medical conditions in newborns in her own practice, which bothered her greatly. The only common denominator she found was that all the babies had been born to parents in the same area of the state of Washington...the Palouse. She mentioned three deliveries in which she saw a mongoloid, a stillbirth and a terribly deformed newborn child all in the same week. She probably conferred with her peers and no doubt found that other physicians had begun observing similar, or at the very least, a more frequent occurrence of birth defects.

She made no connection between the conditions she had observed and Hanford itself, but she did warn my mother, "tongue in cheek," "not to eat anything that came from the ground nearby." She wondered about the "noxious" fumes going up the Hanford smokestacks, as there were rumors that chemicals were being created at Hanford. She also wondered about fluoride and plutonium in the same water source, the Columbia River, after she learned that a study out of the University of Rochester, which had been published in the American Journal of Dentistry, *had been subsequently "censored by the Atomic Energy Commission in the name of national security."*

William remembers hearing her talk to Dr. Blanchard about Hanford's air quality, but could not recall the circumstances of the conversation. Surely, it wasn't the only time she mentioned her concerns. Others must have thought about the safety of those living in the area.

Aunt Margaret witnessed Joe and Delores Parsons' son's thymus condition and saw many more thymus conditions before she retired from her practice. Because the government refused to admit that the facility was responsible for any radioactive or chemical releases into the surrounding areas and because they refused to correct any of the problems, thousand of residents living downwind and downstream of the site were exposed to elevated doses of radiation and increased exposure to the noxious chemicals.

Today, we know that the Hanford Nuclear Reservation is one of the most dangerously polluted places on the planet. But it wasn't until 1986, in response to public pressure and efforts of a citizen group called The Health Education Action League, that the U.S. Department of Energy released more than 19,000 pages of previously classified documents revealing the huge releases of radioactive material that had contaminated the surrounding area and had entered into the Columbia River.

The report refers to ionizing radiation, the type of high-energy radiation capable of causing serious damage to living cells, cellular death and genetic mutation. Hanford Downwinders and those living on the Palouse revealed a significant preponderance of all types of cancers, including thyroid cancer, central nervous system neoplasms, breast, colon, and female reproductive cancers, thyrotoxicosis including hyperthyroidism, Graves' disease and toxic goiter. Additionally, many Downwinders suspected radiation associations with increased incidence of unusually high numbers of spontaneous abortions, infant mortality and birth defects.

In addition to the effects of radiation from inadequately warehoused radioactive materials, strong evidence suggested that the many highly toxic chemicals used at Hanford had also negatively impacted the health of Downwinders.

Although Aunt Margaret had clues as to what might be going on behind the concrete walls of Hanford, she, like the rest of Richland's population, never questioned to what the government was actually exposing its citizens. The people of the state of Washington were proud to house the source of the end of World War II. So patriotic were the residents of Richland that they nicknamed their children's high school "the Bombers." Hanford provided jobs and those jobs brought more money into southeastern Washington. After the war ended, people just wanted to get on with their lives, raise their children and enjoy life. They never suspected that the Hanford Reservation could eventually cause them pain and anguish.

Children who grew up in Richland never asked each other what their fathers did. Day after day, workers went through multiple checkpoints to reach their worksites. Wives were instructed to leave the bedroom if their husbands talked in their sleep, and each individual worker was familiar with only the tiny bit of the project on which he or she was working. Ironically, we now know that while the individuals working on the project had little knowledge of its purpose, Joseph Stalin was kept up to date with all nuclear secrets thanks to Donald Maclean and his fellow agents who constantly fed him the latest data.

In 1995, the 50th anniversary of the war's end, newspapers, radio, television and magazines were filled with memories of that time. Thanks to our father's publication of our family's wartime history in the book Letters from Brackham Wood, *we are able to experience our own family history during those war years. The book has recently taken on a new life, causing all five of Margaret and Moira's children to be interviewed. Some of us were asked to deliver lectures as part of the 50-year festivities.*

The five of us are technically cousins but we refer to one another as brothers and sisters. We have always maintained a close relationship. Since I am the only one of the five who remained in Spokane, I organize our family reunions with the help of my daughters-in-law. We revisit our old haunts and talk non-stop for two weeks nearly every summer. Our family now includes four generations. The Newman Lake cottage has remained in the family for well over seventy years and is the gathering spot for our reunions. What was once a very small cabin has morphed into a summer home in which we can all find a place to lay our heads.

William Walker was a political commentator and television journalist. He worked with ABC News as a consultant. Four years later, he was offered a job as ABC's correspondent covering the Senate and the House of Representatives. At the time of his retirement, he worked as a White House correspondent for ABC News. His wife was also a journalist. They have a son and a daughter and four grandchildren and two great-grand children.

Dr. Bert Walker retired as Professor Emeritus of Epidemiology at the University of Washington. He graduated Summa Cum Laude from Northwestern University with a Bachelor's Degree in Biological Sciences in 1951. He completed his MD degree at Northwestern University in 1955 and was awarded a residency at the University of Washington. Upon completion of his Ph.D. studies in Public Health in 1962, he continued to teach and conduct research at the University of Washington. In 1982, he retired and took a position with the World Health Organization. He and his wife have a son, a granddaughter and two great-grand children. He still loves to lecture. For each of our reunions, he prepares a presentation on something he thinks we should know. We all "go back to school" at Newman Lake for a couple of hours every summer. It's the only time during our gathering that we are "serious."

Catherine Walker Sears is a 1955 graduate of Wellesley College. A talented performer, she appeared in several off-Broadway productions, most of which we siblings attended. Later becoming interested in politics, she volunteered in John F. Kennedy's presidential campaign where she met her future husband, James W. Sears, III. Catherine is a community activist in Hartford, Connecticut, and the founder of The Children's Musical Theater for Underprivileged Youth. She and her husband have three daughters and three granddaughters.

Keiko and I are still very close though our lives have taken very different paths. Our many relocations early in life ignited in Keiko a love of travel that continues to this day. She picked up the Japanese language with very little study even though neither of us had spoken it much at all after we left our home at ages five and seven. When she reached college, she found other foreign languages very easy to learn. Besides Japanese, she now speaks fluently in French, German, and Spanish.

Keiko calls Langley, Virginia, her home but her work as a translator has taken her all over the world. Until she retired, every summer's gathering included a travelogue which captivated us with stories of where she has been and what she has heard. When our children were young she brought age appropriate souvenirs to each of them and taught them games from other countries. She never married, but has continued to fill her life with travel.

We siblings followed her early travels with interest. We frequently found that they correlated with a subsequent political crisis in that part of the world. Journalist William particularly still enjoys teasing her about these coincidences. She takes his interest with good humor but never confirms nor denies his hypotheses.

I became fascinated with history while at college and chose it as a major. I have done research for various agencies and occasionally have helped my husband, Max, investigate insurance claims. My first love, however, is books and I worked for years with Mother in her long-dreamed-of bookshop. Her ability to remember everyone's name, family story and preferences in reading material was a huge boost to our business. During the last five years of the bookstore's life, we opened a teashop in one corner, serving only tea and simple sweets and savories.

Our inspiration to add this part of the business came from the lovely china cups and saucers that were being sold at reasonable prices by the women of my generation who had inherited them from their mothers. They had gone out of fashion, and had been replaced by matching sets of china and casual dinnerware.

Max and I have two sons: Ben and Alex, who have provided us with two grandchildren.

Margaret and my mother are gone now but they remained engaged in the world around them as long as they were alive. They continued to enjoy reading and conversation. Aunt Margaret did not remarry. Upon retirement, she continued her work with the underserved. My mother's spirit seemed to dim for a time after our father passed and for a short time we worried about her. She talked about him a great deal, which has helped in our attempt to unravel their history. She cherished every day they had together and yet, unlike many of her widowed friends, she adjusted to life without him.

She taught Ecclesiastical Embroidery at St. John's Cathedral and also at St. Mark's in Seattle. She and Aunt Margaret traveled together several times. At 85, they returned to Brackham Wood. My mother remarked that, "some things never change." She found the daughters of her village friends, but alas, all of her friends had passed on. Before my father died, he, Mother and Margaret went to Egypt. Scarabs were brought back as gifts for their grandchildren.

My mother and Aunt Margaret were always a great pair. After my father was gone, they lived in adjoining houses in a gated community where they had tea together every day. They were welcome at all family gatherings. Toward the end of their lives they no longer chose to join us at the Lake, but did attend the annual family picnic in Manito Park. For the rest of the time they preferred to visit with us family by family and person by person in their homes. They kept a toy box for the youngest children and games and puzzles for the older ones. They moved around with care but their minds remained as sharp as tacks.

We once tried to delight them with a surprise party. We should have known better. Aunt Margaret's wide circle of friends, colleagues and acquaintances considerably lowered the odds of this possibility. She had heard from several sources that we would be there sometime during the coming month. She and my mother, realized that it was meant to be a surprise and decided to go along with the ruse. However, in the end, Mother's skill as a super-recognizer got the best of us.

On the day that the family was arriving, the five o'clock television news program reported that the airport was closed for a few hours. As one of the reporters interviewed a woman waiting to catch a flight, Mother caught a glimpse of Catherine sitting in the background. She assumed that her niece had arrived earlier and was waiting for the others. She phoned Margaret who could not resist the urge to call a cab. She persuaded Mother to join the greeting party. Our surprise party for them was turned upside down.

Research into our family's WWII and Cold War activities remains as interesting as ever. At last summer's gathering, William's wife, Gemma, surprised us each a with gift copy of a book entitled: My Five Cambridge Friends *written by Yuri Modin, the Soviet agent who had handled all five of the Cambridge spies.*

In the book, written in 1995, Modin describes an American journalist, named Russell, who had none of the "American bombast" and who helped him acclimate to the British way of doing things. Modin described how they exchanged information that he felt was mutually beneficial. Russell also took Modin to the exclusive Athenaeum Club where his knowledge of the British improved by leaps and bounds.

Since this story closely mirrored one contained in Mother's letter to Margaret written on November 20, 1947, we all now wonder if the real name of "Russell" was none other than that of my father's...Thomas Walker.

What was Thomas Walker really doing? William, Bert, Catherine, Keiko and I hope that we have instilled in our children a desire to discover the truth.

THE END

ABOUT THE AUTHORS

 Rita Gard Seedorf is a retired professor who became reacquainted with her high school classmate, Margaret Verhoef, as they worked on planning their 50th high school reunion. Together they began writing their first book historical mystery: *Letters From Brackham Wood,* which was set in WWII England and America. Before entering the world of fiction she wrote two school histories: *A History of the Campus School at Eastern Washington University* and *One Room Out West: The Story of the Jore School and its Students.* She and her husband Marty have a son, a daughter and two grandsons and live in Cheney Washington.

 Margaret Albi Verhoef is a retired teacher and school librarian who became reacquainted with her high school classmate, Rita Seedorf, as they worked on planning their high school reunion. Together they soon began writing *Letters From Brackham Wood.* Margaret, the wife of a retired Army Dental Officer, developed her skills as a letter-writer during the years they were stationed from Alaska to Texas and New York to Washington State. She and her husband Doug have a daughter and a granddaughter and live in Spokane, WA.

www.ingramcontent.com/pod-product-compliance
Lightning Source LLC
Chambersburg PA
CBHW020316260626
47156CB00004B/1241